IF

Magsie Hamilton Little

First published in the United Kingdom in 2018
by Max Press, London

10 9 8 7 6 5 4 3 2 1

Edition no 1, first printing

Text © 2018 by M Hamilton Little
Design and layout © 2018 by Max Press

ISBN: 978 1 906251 86 4

Printed in the United Kingdom

For Private Edward Arthur Briggs

With the Usual Apologies

If you can drink the beer the Belgians sell you,
And pay the price they ask with ne'er a grouse,
If you believe the tales that some will tell you,
And live in mud with ground sheet for a house,
If you can live on bully and a biscuit,
And thank your stars that you've a tot of rum,
Dodge whizzbangs with a grin, and as you risk it
Talk glibly of the pretty way they hum,
If you can flounder through a C.T. nightly
That's three-parts full of mud and filth and slime,
Bite back the oaths and keep your jaw shut tightly,
While inwardly you're cursing all the time,
If you can crawl through wire and crump holes reeking
With feet of liquid mud, and keep your head
Turned always to the place which you are seeking,
Through dread of crying you will laugh instead,

If you can fight a week in Hell's own image,

And at the end just throw you down and grin,

When every bone you've got starts on a scrimmage,

And for a sleep you'd sell your soul within,

If you can clamber up with pick and shovel,

And turn your filthy crump hole to a trench,

When all inside you makes you itch to grovel,

And all you've had to feed on is a stench,

If you can hang on just because you're thinking

You haven't got a chance in ten to live,

So you will see it through, no use in blinking

And you're not going to take more than you give,

If you can grin at last when handing over,

And finish well what you had well begun,

And think a muddy ditch a bed of clover,

You'll be a soldier one day, then, my son.

PART I
1913–1914

Chapter 1

A young man, wearing a hat and clutching a case, stopped at the crossroads to listen. A *clairsach*, an ancient Gaelic stringed instrument reminiscent of a small harp, welcomed the advent of spring as it echoed in the low haze above the mansion block.

It was a Saturday evening in March 1913.

Now that he had arrived, he felt no urge to ascend the stairs to the smart apartment and to engage in small talk with so many strangers with whom he would have so little in common.

The young man listened to the soft, lilting arpeggios of the harp as they wafted towards him but, despite their magical beauty, decided that it would be preferable to spend the last light of this heady day strolling along the wide pathway that ran along the Thames.

Turning his back on the large Victorian, red-brick building where the Professor lived, he glimpsed his reflection in one of the wide, sparkling windows, and paused. He leaned forward a little, as though studying a specimen in a laboratory.

His face did not look too bad. The cold days had left it paler than usual, but the blue-grey eyes did not look as bloodshot. The sandy hair, gently wavy, was still boyish in its cut. The nose was straight, the neck slim; the jaw with its straight, firm line suggested precision.

After lingering a few seconds longer in front of the glinting shield he tightened his hold on his violin, and carried on.

A dark grey suit, a little frayed, but still presentable, covered his athletic frame. All of life stretched ahead of him. He had just completed his studies at the Imperial College and was working, for the time being, in the cashiers' department of London County and Westminster Bank in the city.

With a puff of his cigarette, Edward strolled on, passing the sign of the Eight Bell, which tinkled gently as it swayed in the breeze.

On the Albert Bridge the tollbooths were deserted. Timber was being loaded onto barges and, from time to time, a lad, dressed in breeches ran past breathlessly. What lovers' trysts would take place there that night, in that exact same spot where he was walking?

On the opposite bank, among a confused and crowded mass of rooftops and gable ends, the windows of a sawmill caught the sunlight, perfectly cut, square-edged diamonds, evenly spaced as if set by a master jeweler, and not two miles away in the city docks ships waited to transport the dreams of an empire.

The cool tranquility lay diffused, golden and rippling in the reflection of the river. Edward stopped and stood motionless, watching the glistening water, wondering what currents drove it, and what tides would push him inevitably and inexorably onwards.

It had been such a wonderful year. Only yesterday he had met with the Rutherford's Italian nanny. He recalled that kiss, enveloped in a mist of her strong, sweet eau de cologne and them promptly dismissed the memory.

With a sudden dim feeling, he imagined life extending

predictably and relentlessly before him. At school he had wanted to pass his exams with an almost reckless impatience. Later, as a music student, he had assumed that once he had passed his exams, somehow a set of imaginary doors would open to him, and a world would be placed before him filled with adventure and beautiful women. Yet here he was, lacking the inspiration even to relight his cigarette, which by now had gone out.

He stopped in his tracks, sweeping aside all thoughts of his family. He placed his case on the ground, leaned against the low wall that edged the riverbank, and looked up.

Harry Lloyd was striding towards him.

'Edward!' Lloyd, still a few yards off, was carrying his own odd-shaped case. Edward was used to seeing him, red-faced and bulging-eyed, blowing at his trumpet. He was an apprentice at a stockbroker – and now, as Edward surveyed his old friend's unusually shiny cheeks, it only reminded him of his own inability to make anything happen in his life.

Lloyd's trilby, worn cocked on one side, gave him an air of style, but his stiff white collar was lost about his thin neck with its protruding Adam's apple, and a little misplaced, which told of the young man's efforts to secure it. His striped trousers were a little too long, as if he were still growing into them, and of a thick weave a tad hot for this time of year.

'Are you coming?' he asked. Lloyd seemed relieved to have found someone to accompany him to the party.

'Not sure,' said Edward, glancing across the river.

'Really? Why is that? There will be beautiful girls.'

Edward managed a weak smile at Lloyd. 'I'd rather not,' he sighed.

'Right,' replied Lloyd, ignoring his friend and grabbing

his arm. 'Come on. We'll stay for a bit and look at the women. Then we shall leave.'

'Ten minutes,' said Edward. He did owe the Professor a favour. It was thanks to his introductions that Edward had been able to take on pupils, the income from which paid for his lodgings. Still, as they turned, he couldn't help noticing how the sky had dimmed, a harbinger perhaps of what awaited them.

The two young men had met Professor Frederick Coberg at the Art's Club. The elderly scientist was a kind-hearted patron and ardent music lover. He and his wife were from Bonn, and in London Helga sat on the committees of all the local amateur music groups.

Having checked the apartment number with the porter at the entrance lobby, the two young men began up the staircase. Lloyd paused after the first flight. 'Just a second.' He straightened his tie and hesitated, as if suddenly wondering if he had misinterpreted the dress code on the invitation that read 'smart'.

The Professor's apartment was on the first floor. Strewn about the entrance hall like confetti petals were hats, caps and parasols. Instrument cases, some peculiar-shaped, with great bulbs and protuberances, formed a small mountain in the corner. Edward placed his instrument case among the pile. He lingered a moment at the mirror, placed his hat on the hook, fished out his small tortoiseshell comb from his breast pocket and ran it through his golden hair. He adjusted the navy silk handkerchief in the outside pocket of his jacket.

Behind the heavy oak door the long, smoky drawing room rebounded with low hums and excited squeals. The hostess welcomed the two men and they shook every one of the hot and cold, stiff and flabby hands that were offered to them by way of introduction. There must have been at least twenty faces that blurred and intermingled.

Edward turned around to find he had lost Harry who, leaning on the lid of the Steinway, striking a pose he believed to be debonaire, was deep in conversation with a short, mousy-haired girl he recognized as Kitty Smith. Gauchely he edged into the corner and attempted to blend with it.

The room was packed and Edward was its prisoner. From his low-profile position he could see a small huddle of elderly ladies, their silvery buns bent towards each other. A frail, elegant woman was seated over by the window, the most airy, comfortable place. Someone addressed her as Princess and she held out her hand, her dark eyes darting constantly, as she aimed her reflex smile at whomever she was addressing. A stout gentleman stood fixed at her side.

Across the room two young girls sat together on a chaise longue, one fair-haired and the other a brunette. Edward could not quite make out their faces, which were concealed by hats. A dapper, blond teenage boy, sitting on the arm of the couch, was chatting to the fair-haired girl, and puffing smoke from his cigarette into the air outside. Edward could tell by the cut of his suit that it was expensive, at which thought he felt a twinge of envy.

'Would you like a cocktail?' The voice belonged to a handsome lad who must have been no more than eighteen, although he looked more like twelve.

'No thank you,' said Edward. 'I'm fine.'

'Please,' said the lad, waving the drink in Edward's face. 'It's one of my aunt Helga's creations.'

Edward took the glass awkwardly and carried it to a lady in a pink straw hat, who was talking to a ruddy-faced man with a flamboyant moustache.

Propped against the wall, Edward continued to survey the room from his corner, while the Professor's wife buzzed from one cluster of people to another, settling briefly at each. He couldn't help noticing her generous girth and pendulous bosom were kept in order by a strict undergarment. Her lipstick had moved, and her eyebrows and lashes were snowy with powder. She flitted restlessly about, just in case anyone was feeling left out, so that she could include them.

He remembered hearing that her hope had once been to have a salon, but since her husband's connections were limited her guests were not always selected from families she would have liked, with all the social advantages they might bring.

By 8.30 some musicians had plotted their escape. As the throng began to thin, the dapper Mr Lenz shook hands with the fair-haired girl sitting on the chaise longue, but to Harry's dismay, there was absolutely no sign of Gustav Holst.

'Are you going play?' Professor Coberg begged a baffled Sir Archibald, who was promptly ushered to the piano stool. After a lively cadence, he cleared his throat. A fine rendition of 'Love Is Mine' was followed by a respectful moment's silence, then a burst of clapping and suitably impressed murmuring.

Kitty Smith expressed a wish to hear 'Danny Boy', but by the time Professor Coberg had made his way to the other side of the room with his target in clear sight, his victim had already snuck out, along with a long, steady stream of others.

There were just twenty or so guests left when Kitty, who was still chatting to Harry, was also making her excuses as she let slip that she had come all the way from

Berkshire in the hope of hearing Helga sing.

Harry emitted an audible sigh of relief and exchanged knowing glances with Edward, who was also edging towards the door.

'Well,' protested a somewhat flustered Helga. 'I have forgotten the words!' but the resistance was weak and in vain, as the small group insisted, their voices united in chorus, the lad and the pretty maid included. With pink cheeks, Kitty took her place next to Sir Archibald and the piano, and a hushed silence descended. In a wavering tone, she sang feelingly, her eyes tight shut. She reached for the notes and, having not quite hit them, hummed in their vicinity.

The girl sitting on the chaise longue put her gloved hand in her mouth as if trying to hide it, and her friend looked askance as if she, too, was struggling. Meanwhile, Harry Lloyd stood, hands in his pockets, having forgotten to look elegant, aghast and flushed.

Helga, on the other hand, seemed oblivious to any embarrassment. A dozen eyes were focused on her, and she was enjoying herself as she reached the agonizingly flat C sharp.

When, at last, it was over everyone applauded, colluding in the lie. 'You see, your Highness,' said Helga, turning to the gracious elderly lady at the window, 'I told you I was rusty.'

'It was beautiful, darling,' replied the lady, though with a different emotion than Helga understood.

'Have you by any chance brought your violin?' asked the Professor, turning to Edward.

Seized by panic, Edward felt his heart thump. 'I'll just get it,' he said. Once in the hallway he lifted his hat off the hook, picked up his case and was about to make his exit when a hush descended among the crowd and another instrument began.

He turned, glancing through the doorway to study the elegant *clairsach*, but almost immediately his gaze averted to its player, glimpsing in the dappled gaslight the young girl with the chestnut hair who had been sitting beside her companion on the chaise longue and talking to Jasper Lenz.

She appeared completely at ease as her white fingers fluttered across the strings, darting occasionally towards the levers, and her chest lifted and fell. Her light bronze hair shone duskily and her heart-shaped face looked content, her lips slightly open, her eyebrows raised a little, her cheeks faintly blushing. There was something intriguing about her. He assumed that, like him, she was another of the Professor's protégés. She certainly could captivate an audience.

Suddenly, Edward found himself back inside the room.

On this occasion the adoring sighs and resounding applause were genuine.

'Beautiful,' gushed the Professor, who had been so moved by the music that he was dabbing his eyes with his handkerchief.

'You play very nicely, my dear,' added Helga. 'Do you take lessons?'

The girl, who did not appear comfortable with flattery, began to blush as she put her instrument away carefully into its leather case. She hardly heard Helga's next question. Ever so politely, she excused herself.

On the staircase Edward caught up with her. 'If you'll permit me,' he said. 'May I help you?'

It was her fair-haired friend who answered. 'How kind.'

'Do you play as well?' he asked.

'Oh no, Alice is the musical one.'

Edward picked up the black leather case which was not as heavy as he expected and as the door closed, the two girls, arms linked, proceeded to walk not downwards but upwards, followed by a somewhat breathless Edward, carrying two instruments, one in each hand.

Meanwhile, Harry Lloyd, who had resumed his fashionable gait, hastened after Kitty Smith in the opposite direction.

After a few steps Evangeline turned around.

'Goodbye,' she said, and laughed a light, bright laugh that made her eyes twinkle.

A somewhat confused Edward looked back at her.

'This is where I live,' she added, making for the other side of the landing.

'And do you live here as well?' Edward asked, turning to Alice.

Alice shook her head. 'No,' she said, 'I'm over there.' She pointed to another door, further along and a few steps up.

Together they trod the dozen paces that separated the two doors. Edward tried to think of something inspiring or interesting to say, but the words evaded him.

'Well, thank you and good night,' said Alice in a demure, well-mannered tone that any girl might use for a man she had just met and expected never to see again.

'Not at all,' he said, so quickly that the words as they spilled out sounded almost abrupt.

In the few short moments needed for the door to open and for him to put down the instrument case, he glimpsed inside through the narrow, oak-panelled hallway to where a door opened into a large reception room. There were several pieces of tasteful antique furniture and a piano. To the other side of the hall a table was set for dinner. There, an elderly gentleman in a linen suit and wearing gold spectacles sat engrossed in a newspaper.

All these impressions were fleeting, since the door closed almost immediately. Edward stood silently before making his way down. Once in the street, he glanced up to the windows of the second floor and tried to guess the number of rooms in the apartment, before walking on, lost in thought. It occurred to him that Jasper had been talking to Alice before he had left and he wondered if they were lovers.

He began down the street, his violin tucked under his arm once again, his head spinning. On the way he bought sausages, and by the time he reached home he had entirely forgotten the pretty harpist who played the instrument of an angel.

Chapter 2

Beneath the dappled shade of silver maples bathing caps bobbed in the water of the Serpentine like bright anemones. Crocuses had begun to sprout and the noon light wove gilt circles on the grass. Everything felt new and shiny. Children played, oblivious to the solitary cloud that lingered, or the specks of the swallows that glided happily towards the unknown.

Edward arrived near the stone bridge and settled on a seat with his newspaper. He flicked cursorily through the opening pages, ignoring what Mr Asquith had to say about the Pankhurst woman, and was just folding the thin paper in two when a young man appeared from the direction of the Round Pond, chatting happily to the girl in a peach summer dress who walked with him.

Recognizing Alice straight away and almost simultaneously identifying the man walking with her as Jasper Lenz, he straightened the crumpled page, his heart pounding to the accompaniment of its crinkling and rustling. Still camouflaged by his newspaper, he allowed them to pass. Their pace appeared to be so hurried it seemed to him they must be late for something.

Reflecting back to the night he had met Alice, it struck him that he had not once seen her at the Professor's events. Concluding she was not one of his protégés at all, but a society girl, the thought crossed his mind that he had never kissed one of those. It wouldn't be like kissing the

Rutherford's nanny, without the uphill struggle called courtship. That long, curious road, littered with charming compliments, whispered suggestions and meaningful looks might just as easily lead nowhere, for Alice was a nice girl and everyone knew that with nice girls it was less straightforward. What was less certain was how they kissed, and whether the rumours were true that they would allow you to go further.

He strode briskly back to his office, consumed by reflection. In the balmy sunlight his dizzy heart gradually resumed its normal rhythm.

That evening, he turned over in his bed. Two or three times he moved the small cotton pillow beneath his head, but it was no use. Opening his eyes, he formed pictures from the light and shadows cast by the window. Something had changed, though he could not say exactly what. He had led an uneventful life, but now it occurred to him that he had become oddly sensitive.

Over the days that followed he began to take an interest in small, apparently insignificant details, such as the intoxicating words of a poem. If a woman passed, he would gaze wistfully after her, drinking in her perfume, and he practised slow ballads, languishing in their melancholy. Perhaps he was in love. But no, this was not love. Not with Alice or anyone else. He was in love with love itself.

At the realization of this fact he grew ashamed of his immaturity. At night in his imagination he painted that enchanting face he could not dismiss, with every brush stroke reminding himself of its subtleties – the full yet delicate mouth slightly turned up at the edges, the large, dark eyes whose shade couldn't quite be captured, the tiny dent between the brows, and the small dimples in the cheeks in the formation of the smile. Only then, in the moment of that expression, could he see everything with clarity, as those large eyes crumpled into crescent moons and the silky warmth of the voice enveloped him. He had met prettier girls, but no one had ever affected him in the same way.

For several weeks this uneasy, infantile twilight filled with images of her continued. He obsessed about her constantly, interrupted only by the usual irritating duties, such as calling his parents or going to his office job.

It was the middle of July before, on a boiling hot day, the Professor sent another invitation to one of his social events. This time, when the envelope fell upon the doormat, Edward rushed to it. He picked it up and tore open the seal. He read the scribbled words out loud: 'Helga and I should love it if you were to come for tea next Sunday.' He wrote back his acceptance immediately.

When Sunday finally arrived, in a state of excited nervousness, he washed and shaved. He polished his shoes. He went through his collars and cuffs, picking out the best one. Leaving extra time, he set off along his familiar route from Cornwall Gardens, making the usual detour along the Embankment, just as he had done before.

As he walked, he hummed, noticing the downy thistle balls of wind that came to rest on the water of the River Thames. The waves jostling on the surface had all but vanished and the water had become a mirror. Somewhere a gate was being painted and the heady cocktail of turpentine eddied in the air. The light darted on the brass balls on the wrought iron railings, and around polished, handsome front doors wafted the fresh, earthy aroma of newly cut grass.

Shortly before four, he rang the Professor's doorbell, smartly turned out in his crisp linen suit.

Ivy stood in exactly the same spot as when Harry Lloyd had ogled her, wearing the same little white cap and apron, but there were only a few items decorating the hallway and no instrument cases, just a small collection of boaters, fedoras and panamas.

Edward entered the crowded drawing room, glancing around expectantly, but there was not a single familiar face in sight except the boy who had offered him a drink at the Coberg's last party. In the corner where he had taken refuge previously two bald gentlemen were engaged in earnest conversation. His gaze drifted over the heads to where Hugh and Albert Green were about to sing a duet. Kitty Smith was sitting on the piano stool, chatting to the Professor, and on the chaise longue where Alice and Evangeline had once sat, a huddle of plump ladies had squeezed together and were tucking into cake.

Alone with his disappointment, Edward walked to the hallway, picked up his hat and peered up the staircase towards Alice's floor. Pausing momentarily, he turned and continued downwards.

Once outside in the street he glanced up at the windows, but saw only closed curtains. For no valid reason he felt cheated. The flame in his ingenuous heart had been snuffed out, a desire for love and fulfillment that he had awaited for so long in the form of a young russet-haired woman who played the harp. He straightened his tie and strode back into the cocoon of his routine, a refuge that the folly of the last couple of months had stolen from him.

It was a boiling hot day in July before the wheels of destiny forced that opinion to change.

Bank was a congested intersection, thronged in every direction by motor vehicles. Somewhere located between the corner of Bank of England and those of the Royal

Exchange and the Mansion House building stood the most influential square mile of the most talked about city in the world. Here lay the real jewel of the Empire, the core of the global economy, the beating heart of the known universe.

Every day a stampede of suited men arrived in this spot fresh from their routine commute along the electrified Metropolitan line to sit behind desks and ledgers. At five o'clock they made their way home again, while not a mile away another army of workers and shipmen, black from soot and dirt, toiled to support their families in the sweatshops, factories, shipyards and docklands.

Umbrella in one hand, briefcase in the other, Edward began his familiar route home on foot. The day was still hot and he was sweating. He was not thinking of anything particular as he paced along Oxford Street. Nor did he particularly notice the women who harangued the passers-by at Speaker's Corner. Passing by a wooden bench, he was suddenly struck by the memory of the beautiful, gentle, easy smile that had belonged to Alice. Perhaps, he thought to himself now, she might have left London.

Harry had formed an attachment with Kitty Smith. Sometimes he confided in Edward, when his happiness met with unspoken envy. Edward did not begrudge his friend; instead, Harry's swoons and glazed, puppy-dog eyes offered hope, even as the day arrived for the Art's Club summer revue.

Kitty, who looked elegant in a kimono-style tea gown and a silk scarf, sat expectantly in the front row of chairs. She was looking forward to seeing Harry play his oboe. The stage was set with chairs and music stands, and by half past six the audience was gathering in the foyer and eager ladies, having bought their tickets in advance, had already taken their places. The orchestra was seated and a hushed silence descended. Fighting to regain his composure, Edward clung to the neck of his violin, wishing he had put in the hours of practice required, rather than the occasional run-throughs he had managed in actuality.

Afterwards, Sir Archibald accepted the floral bouquet with a mixture of delight and astonishment. The applause subsided and Edward's eyes skimmed the various huddles of the audience, alighting on a group he recognized.

It was Harry Lloyd who, ruddy-faced from blowing his oboe and dabbing a cotton handkerchief over his forehead, made eye contact with Evangeline and then in the blur of clapping hands, Edward glimpsed Alice. He laid his fiddle into its blue velvet bed, carefully placing the bow into its slot in a state of excitement.

Half an hour later the two groups came face to face.

'Good evening,' trilled Evangeline. As she held out her hand, Alice's gaze grew less remote. Extending her own hand, she appeared to flush a little, but Edward knew that meant nothing.

Standing beside her was yet another familiar face. It was the lad at the party who had offered him a drink. 'Tonight I am their chaperone,' grinned Hugh, shaking Edward's hand first, and then Harry's.

The two girls linked arms, heads together, talking and laughing. Edward watched their four slim ankles as they began down the street.

'Why weren't you at the Professor's the other day?' He blurted out the words without thinking.

'Helga gossiped about us.'

'Don't be rude about my dear aunt!' called out Hugh.

The two girls, arms still linked, stopped in their tracks and turned.

'Your aunt is a fine woman,' said Harry, and then everyone laughed.

'Where are you off to now?' asked Edward, trying to make the question sound casual.

'Home,' Alice answered.

'Would you like to come up and have a cup of tea?' said Evangeline. 'Alice is inviting you.'

Edward glanced at Alice. 'Are you?'

'Of course.' She spoke warmly, tidying an errant dark gold curl behind her ear.

Harry spotted Kitty Smith walking along the opposite side of Old Church Street and made his excuses, while the others hailed a motor cab.

Any bashfulness among the group soon gave way towards relaxed cheerfulness and Hugh's anecdotes ensured that the journey passed quickly. He was at school in Windsor. He loved music, but he was not a musician. Alice had tried diligently to teach him to play the piano once – but he had two left hands and almost immediately she had been forced to give up.

At Alice's apartment a woman took their coats. She was swan-necked and high-browed, her grey, wispy hair swept into a hairstyle that reminded Edward of his mother's. It was not obvious whether she was a servant or a relative.

'Good evening, Rose,' said Evangeline.

'Is grandfather home?' she asked.

'His lordship is in the library,' Rose answered in a lilting, soft Scottish accent took their hats and Edward helped Alice with her coat. A ginger cat, detecting the smell of strangers, slunk into view behind her, turned up its tail and padded off.

To the right of the hall was a large walnut desk. A haze of tobacco smoke haloed the gas lamp that stood on the leather top and which emitted a golden light. The same snowy-bearded, bespectacled gentleman whom Edward had seen all those months ago rose from his captain's chair, a lighted pipe in his hand. Alice glided over to him and, throwing her arms around his neck, kissed him on the cheek.

'Was it a good concert?' Fondly, the elderly gentleman touched Alice's cheek, William Purefoy did not seem to notice the others standing in the dining room. His face was kind, and a natural bonhomie warmed his stone-coloured eyes. His head reminded Edward of the portrait of Nicolaes Ruts, a fur merchant painted by Rembrandt, with a deeply furrowed brow that suggested profound meditation, and wisdom.

As the reflective, watery eyes fell upon Edward, they became questioning. Edward bowed low and, in a somewhat nervous voice, introduced himself.

Alice chipped in. 'Edward plays the violin.'

William reclaimed his hand and his bushy eyebrows lifted.

'Like grandmother used to,' she added quickly, glancing at the others who were chatting among themselves behind her in the dining room.

'Are you the son of Albert Sanderson?' asked Alice's grandfather, smiling courteously and studying Edward.

'We met at the Professor's,' explained Alice, her cheeks glowing.

'Well, I wish you a lovely evening,' said her grandfather, addressing both of them. And with that, pipe still in hand, he wandered back to the library.

A second door led off the dining room to the drawing room, with its elegant, fine oil paintings, understated chic furniture and the harp.

The girls retired to the room that opened out from this one on to a conservatory. At the threshold, Alice turned to Edward: 'Do smoke if you like.' We are just going to take off our hats.'

'They are quite special, those two,' sighed Hugh, sitting down on the deep, wide Chesterfield sofa. Edward sat down opposite him in the wing-backed fireside chair. He wasn't interested in Evangeline.

'Is Alice engaged to Jasper Lenz?' he asked, lighting up a cigarette.

'What makes you think that?'

'It was just an impression…'

Hugh played with the silver cufflink on his shirtsleeve.

Edward watched with curiosity, as if he were striving to discover the truth, but Hugh's next comment made it obvious he knew no more than Edward: 'I imagine it's possible.'

By the time the girls had returned from freshening up the subject had been left behind and relatively harmless topics such as religion and politics prevailed for at least half an hour.

Edward followed the movements of Alice's long, slender fingers as she poured the tea. In his imagination he painted the outline of her body.

'Well, I think I should be going,' said Evangeline at last, yawning, having consulted her wristwatch.

The men stood up.

'Good night, darling,' said Evangeline to Alice. She said a quick goodbye to the men and began along the corridor, where she quickly disappeared.

'May I call on you again?' asked Edward of Alice, as the men walked to the door.

She seemed embarrassed. Turning on her heel, she pecked Hugh affectionately on the cheek, as if he might have been a younger brother.

The thought briefly occurred to Edward that the lad might be in love with Alice, but he did not give that impression and, in any case, he was far too young for her. He reminded Edward of himself at that age, although Hugh had more confidence. He said little of his past or his family.

The two men descended the staircase. Outside the building they shook hands and strode off in different directions into the cool night, their young, free souls beaming with hope, while the universe continued on its fixed, inevitable path.

Chapter 3

Since his retirement from the Royal Navy William Purefoy was happy to hide away in his library. Society bored him these days, and he enjoyed writing. He was in no doubt that *The Problems and Solutions to Western Civilization* was sorely needed in such an uncertain world. He could not understand how so many children growing up these days were unaware of capitalism.

To work, he needed smooth paper, fluid ink and a new, softly gliding pen nib. To prevent making a mess he put a sheet of lined paper underneath. So far he had completed nine chapters, but there remained many more questions to tackle. What would the segregationist policies of the new South Africa do to the Empire? In which direction would Canada face? How would Australia fare with its Asian neighbours? What role did Zionism play in the decaying Ottoman Empire? And what were the implications of California's anti-Japanese legislation?

When not pondering international relations, he would sometimes be found sitting in the Embankment Gardens near the apartment in Carlisle Mansions, inhaling the balmy air and watching the boats as they passed by, or in the Zoological Gardens in Regents Park, where he would enjoy an elephant ride.

It had been fifty-five years since he had married Jennifer Tate. Her father had been a prominent lawyer; her mother was Lady Helena MacLean, the second daughter of a Scottish baronet. They had one daughter, Isobel, who married an inventor who had been much older. Isobel had died in childbirth, a tragedy that cruelly silenced all the gossipmongers who had objected to the age difference of her parents; and it had devastated her father, who, in desperation had turned to gin for solace.

Alice was eight when her father died after a sudden illness. The child had never seen death, but as she saw the inert, frail outline sunken into the bed where it lay, something changed in her. The waxen forehead, its smooth skin taut, the white mouth with dark blue around the edges were images that ingrained themselves into her memory.

From the on she lived with her grandparents in Scotland. It was they who brought Alice up, among the suits of armour, stags' antlers and heavy tapestries that decorated the high oak-panelled walls that smelt of beeswax. It was in one such grand room that Alice learned to speak, and even as a small child she sang. The elderly couple saw in the grandchild the daughter they had lost, and cocooned her in their love and adoration.

From then on she lived with her grandparents. A governess was engaged to teach her languages and mathematics. Rose, who also acted as housekeeper, gave her a *clairsach* one Christmas.

At ten years of age Alice attended a girl's boarding school near Inverness, returning for holidays to the house at Glen Mar. She was sixteen when her grandmother became frail and caught pneumonia. After she died, William and his granddaughter came to live in London and the *clairsach* travelled with them.

Alice was a spirited child, although her comfortable life made few demands of her. Thanks to her family's social position, she moved in the highest echelons, and was taken under the wing of Helga Coberg, who guided and nurtured the young Alice.

Sitting at the dinner table together, William and Alice would eat a simple supper. The night he met Edward was no different.

'How was the concert?' he asked Alice later that evening. He made no mention of Edward and seemed to have hardly registered his friend Harry.

'It was good.' Alice studied a glint in the water glass beside her plate. Images of the evening flitted through her mind, but she failed to make sense of them.

A silence descended that was not awkward, just the familiar rest in conversation between two people at ease with each other, broken only by the tinkling of forks against porcelain and the faint rustle of a napkin, before at last Alice walked over to the instrument that her mother and grandmother had played before her, took her place on the mahogany stool and played.

Later, alone in her room, she undressed, slipped on the shell-pink satin nightdress and stood before the mahogany wardrobe whose stylish, oval mirror reached to the floor. For a few long moments she remained there, motionless, aware of the sweet faint perfume of fresh linen and the Ponds Vanishing Cream she rubbed into her palms.

The shutters were closed. No one else was in the room, and there was no reason to be alarmed. She opened the door and padded barefoot into the drawing room. The harp was safe, but she jumped again at a noise, and a tail brushed past her legs. At that moment she noticed the broken pieces of the Tole vase. She had never really liked it anyway. With a light jerk of her head, she shook her bronze locks over her shoulder and plaited a chunky braid, holding it a little way out. She climbed into bed and pulled the blankets around her ears. Hugging her crisp, cool pillow, she let out a yawn and stretched her toes, her young head filled with Edward. She had noticed his even, brilliant teeth, and his chiseled jaw and followed the movements of his long, artistic fingers as they darted across the neck of his violin. His phrasing was beautifully judged and his tuning perfect. He was a brilliant musician, although he did not appear to be at all conscious of the fact, which made him even lovelier.

Chapter 4

Sitting at the desk in his bachelor flat, Edward gazed vacantly at the patches of grey over the rooftops as they grew dark. A light icing-sugar frost whitened the lawns of the garden squares, and the cobbles on the streets below shone with the damp. The leaves had begun to fall from the trees and the jaded translucence of their branches seemed to reinforce the sense of emptiness.

He turned his mind to Alice and began to think of an excuse to contact her. Almost of its own accord, the fountain pen started to doodle on the correspondence card that he wanted to send to her. As the nib sank into the smooth surface of the paper it struck him that a declaration of his feelings left unsigned would be far easier, but the upholding of etiquette made for a task of much greater complexity and finesse, so that he almost gave up.

Wiping his brow with his free hand, he signed his name with a flourish, stood up and, with narrow eyes, surveyed his effort. Seizing it defiantly with his clammy fingers, he read it again, pacing up and down the room with it, until, with a heavy sigh, he tore the paper in half and flung it into the wastepaper basket. At last, he collapsed into a leather armchair. With a concentrated effort, he studied the flock velvet wallpaper pattern in detail.

What she really thought of him remained a mystery. She gave him no clue as to her true feelings, if, indeed, they actually existed.

If

As the third correspondence card fell to its predicable fate, there came a knock at the door.

'Are you there?' said a voice.

The doorknob turned and a head appeared in the opening fissure. The hat, usually tilted, was straight, the expression more grave than usual.

Edward wondered at first if it was a complaint about poor working conditions that made Harry Lloyd's previously cheerful expression fade. Perhaps work was proving too tiresome for his friend. If New York share prices had fallen, it would easily depress him, but even that was no reason for him to call around unannounced. A woman was the only explanation for that.

Two large whiskies were poured. Glass in one hand, cigarette in the other, Harry flung himself on the Chesterfield and proceeded to blurt out the entire story of his affair with Kitty Smith.

Edward gave a convincing impression of listening attentively. Of course, he was not surprised by any of it. Kitty Smith was one of those women unaware of their own effect on others, who liked to dabble in new experiences, but who were already disillusioned before they had taken the first step.

'Listen, old chap…' Harry repeated his story for the third time. After that, he implored Edward not to tell anyone, on his mother's life, the situation.

Edward agreed without hesitation.

Then Harry said: 'I think I should marry her.'

Edward's eyebrows knitted. 'Steady on,' he said.

The whisky bottle emptied and the square patch of grey behind the rooftops glowed orange. The young men talked on, and the vision of a woman's white body shone in the imagination of both.

When Harry had left, Edward turned to his desk once again, and this time the words flowed freely. Soon afterwards his head dropped on to his shoulders, his tea cold in the china cup that lay on the table beside the armchair. He had told Alice that he loved her.

Just a few streets away the cheery driver of a gleaming burgundy Minerver Tourer creeping in first gear switched on his headlights. In the passenger seat beside him sat Evangeline, on her lap a little white dog. Their affair had begun two weeks earlier, but was already reaching its critical stage, when Evangeline knew she would give herself to him. She also knew that he was married, but the fact did not bother her. She sat, her scarlet coat collar turned up at the chin, and only her nose was visible. Her fur hat was pulled down, so that it almost hid her eyes. Teeth chattering, she awaited developments that she had no power to resist.

Sir Charles Spicer was a man who had established himself. As founder of Spicer Industries, his range of business interests included tobacco, wheat and gasoline, though his real passion was horses. His healthy cheeks and generous girth were borne of a love of luxury and a competitive streak that ensured he would attain those comforts he felt he was entitled to. For two years he had been engaged in his own battle to divorce his wife from whom he was separated, but with terrier-like tenacity she had clung on to the comforts he provided and showed no sign at all of relinquishing the stately pile in Suffolk, or the sophisticated wooden skiing chalet in St Moritz.

For as long as he could remember, he had consoled himself with a succession of beauties, from the most respectable theatres and musical and the most exclusive hotels the British Isles had to offer. In return, he awarded handsomely those who had made his life bearable, but the solace they offered was hollow, and he quickly became bored with their cheap thrills and unsophisticated rhetoric, which lingered on the palette of his *bon viveur* as a sickly, empty taste and leaving him hungry.

That was before fate brought him Evangeline. They met at a dinner, where they were sitting next to each other. To begin with Winter gave the bright young thing who gazed at him with doe-like eyes scarcely a second thought, but having so cursorily dismissed her during the fish course, it began to dawn on him that there was something intriguing about her, something he had never countered in a girl of her age and breeding.

When the port had been served, and as the fine mist of cigar smoke clouded the dining room, he saw clearly the potential in this flirtatious, slightly tipsy child, and a yearning for freedom bordering on recklessness. He was an open-minded man, who had taken advantage of all the revolutionary opportunities modern life had put before him, but his eyes were blind to the seismic changes that were taking place within her.

The roots of the surge lay in her childhood. Even at twelve Evangeline had been painfully aware of what duty and her parents expected of her and with their high expectations she had seen stretching out before her an arid, meaningless destiny. Aware that her looks would not suffice in finding a husband, a sense of pragmatism had been forced upon her; she saw that marriage was a necessity if her fate was not to starve, although she was not a gold digger.

She was not gifted at music like her best friend Alice, and had very limited connections. Maybe if she was lucky she would meet someone suitable at the Henley boating parties; but of all the eligible boys that she countered there and on the Hurlingham tennis courts, there was not a single one she admired. They were all arrogant.

Those large, aquamarine eyes were quite open. The girl who batted their lids knew too well that the only happiness in store for her was at best security. There was no resentment either, only sadness for the father she had lost as a child through a protracted terminal illness; nor did she blame the poor, frail mother who depended on her.

When Evangeline had been placed next to Charles at dinner, it did not once cross her mind that she could find herself attracted to him. She was far more drawn to the dashing, elegant Jasper Lenz, but as the evening wore on she noticed how Charles's warm, open features became animated as he spoke. He exuded a bonhomie that she convinced herself had nothing to do with the sense of wellbeing offered by financial stability. He was mature, and every finger on his strong, manicured hands seemed to promise that he would be able to look after her, although whether he might accept her liberal ideas on voting was another question.

Over the fish course, as the topic of conversation skated over the issue of marriage, Charles protested that he led a monk-like existence since separating from his wife, but Evangeline was having none of it. She divested on the theme of mistresses and indeed the role of women in society in general so confidently and, some might say, outspokenly, that Charles saw in her an unusual quality. She was interested in motor vehicles.

He found to his surprise that he could discuss matters that other girls found tiresome, and he was interested in her views on current affairs. Was the day of imperialism over or just beginning? How would only the second Democratic American president since the civil war deal with the appalling racial divisions of Washington? Was Buenos Aires, with its rampant nationalism and eyes on the Falklands, the future powerhouse of the southern hemisphere or a gilded sham? Her answers were informed.

The exchange of long, meaningful glances grew more frequent. They sat on the corner sofa, shielded by the walnut cabinet that allowed Charles to begin touching Evangeline's hand. Almost accidentally he found himself kissing her ear and then, naturally, her neck. Inevitably, two days later, Evangeline was tucked into the passenger seat of his new motor that was heading back to his rooms at Claridge's and then on to dine at Gambrinus.

Chapter 5

Alice's stomach was taut, her mouth dry. Unable to eat, she sipped tea and flicked through the headlines without paying attention to their messages of doom. It crossed her mind that during the last week she had seen nothing of Evangeline or Jasper or any of her other friends, and, turning things over in her mind, she concluded that whatever it was that was preoccupying them, she would soon get to hear about it. Perhaps they had gone abroad. She could never keep track of anyone these days. Her friends were stray cats, always away at fashionable reviews and glamorous parties in Cannes, Munich or Berlin. Jasper had gone to Paris that summer to buy suits. All the best tailors were based there.

Edward called that afternoon to ask her to accompany him to the Ambassador's Theatre to see *Panthea*. Helga acted as chaperone, but when the motor taxi dropped them in Piccadilly she allowed them to walk together, claiming that she needed to buy a handbag in Fortnum's and would catch up. They strolled ahead, their steps moving in parallel, and Alice gazed up at Edward. Afterwards, she felt excited and heady, and above all, relieved. She knew nothing of his family, but none of it mattered. It was impossible not to love the rhythm of his soul, the way his eyes twinkled when he spoke and the fact that he was kind. There was something about his smile that suggested he would take care of her.

So when Evangeline knocked on the door late that evening, Alice was bursting to tell her everything, but immediately she could tell something was wrong. Evie appeared to be trembling. She was pale and thin, and instead of her usual thick dressing gown she wore a thin silk robe. Clutched in her fingers was a packet of cigarettes.

Alice gave her a quick hug. 'Where have you been?' She tried to sound casual, but Evangeline made a face.

'What do you mean?' she said, slumping on the couch. 'I've been away.' She smiled enigmatically. She said nothing of the fact she had not been abroad at all. She had been at Claridges.

The two girls sat together on the couch, exchanging news of no importance, and Evangeline began to smoke. Her mood seemed strange to Alice, so much so that she felt compelled to ask: 'What on earth's wrong?'

Evangeline looked away.

Mystified, Alice continued to gaze at her friend, but Evangeline would not look at her. She appeared to be anticipating the next question and when asked directly if she was seeing anyone raised her brow and took a long draw at her cigarette. With a light tap she discarded the ash into the silver dish.

Thinking the worst, all thoughts of Edward banished. Alice took her friend's hand. Perhaps there had been an accident, or an illness.

'Well….' After Evangeline blurted it all out she reached for the ashtray, and the long sleeve of her robe slipped back, baring her forearm.

Veiled in cigarette smoke, with a mixture of consternation and excitement, and a little envy, Alice guessed, 'You became a woman?'

Evangeline gazed at the fireplace. Her faraway eyes

mirrored the recollection of an experience that Alice could not possibly understand. She felt bereft. If only she could share with her friend the great, terrifying moment she had experienced. But she could not. Something else had turned her closest friend into a stranger, and that was shame.

Concealing a deep sense of isolation, with the slightest of movements, Evangeline touched her lips with her fingertip, as if the revelation she had just imparted was a stain, something that should be wiped out. Then, with the uttermost composure and deliberation, she tapped the ashtray again.

An uncomfortable silence fell between the two friends. Evangeline's collected, almost icy manner continued to belie the agonizing burden weighing on her.

Evangeline cleared her throat and, heart pounding, fixed her attention again unflinchingly on the marble fireplace, as every second of her time at the hotel flooded back into her memory.

Alice, believing that something dreadful had occurred, didn't dare say anything, and neither could she, for her throat had constricted. Her kind but immature heart ached, her first instinct to call for help, but almost immediately she abandoned the thought, sensing it would be inappropriate.

Coughing so as not to burst out crying, Evangeline's hand broke free. She stretched out her arm and with a little yawn said, 'Well, I should go. Mother will be expecting me.'

She planted a feathery kiss on Alice's forehead and smoothed her cold hand over it.

'Off already?' Alice said softly, struggling to find her own words, for there were none that could mask her own sense of inadequacy.

After Evangeline had gone she undressed quickly and

slipped into her nightgown, absorbed in thought processes that possessed no logic or reason. Torn, she slipped into bed and threw the covers over herself, as if attempting to bury the problem. She could not quite decide whether what had happened to Evangeline was positive or negative, whether she ought to envy or sympathize with her.

She remained wide-eyed, immobile and ignorant. In her mind's eye she saw Evie in a murky room with the haunting shadow of a stranger. From there her mind turned to Edward and his reassuring smile; and after that to his letter, which by now she knew by heart. He loved her – and that knowledge both filled her with heady excitement and a gut-twisting, naked fear. Gazing up at the reflection of the moonlight on the ceiling, she wondered if what had happened that day was a fugitive piece of her own future, in all its strange, unknowable destiny.

It would be five days before Edward called again, and by then ice floated in sheets upon the Thames and along Cheyne Walk. The night's heavy fall muffled the tread of horses' hooves and carriage wheels, silenced the horns and stilled the engines that seemed numbed by it. The street lamps, lit sooner than usual, looked down at all this music of the street with a muted radiance. Through the window of the apartment their dim light shone, its strange shadows spilling on to the piano keyboard and the music stand where a song sat waiting to be sung.

The doors of the Purefoy drawing room were closed, except the one to the library, which was always ajar; but it was empty. Grandfather must have been sleeping or have gone out.

Edward sat upon the couch, arms outstretched, hands splayed, soaking up the fire's heat.

Helga Coberg had just left; her half-empty cup of

coffee sat on the table just where she had put it still warm.

Apart from the trip to the theatre, Edward and Alice had met several times, though they were never alone. There had been another tea at the Professor's, and a number of visits to her apartment, but Grandfather was always working, seated at his desk and Rose bustled in and out. The weather kept away all interruptions.

'Alice…'

Met with silence, Edward murmured the words he had long wanted to say to her, and as soon as he said them he felt a release.

Alice, upon hearing him speak of his feelings, walked to the window, shivering a little from the draught let in by the tiny cracks in the wooden frame. Turning her body slightly towards him, she glanced across, but as soon as their eyes met she quickly looked away. She resisted weakly, held her lips tightly together as if to shield herself from this over-whelming, tender aggressor, but he held her so strongly that almost immediately she gave in. This, her first kiss, was an invasion, her immediate reaction to push him away.

Outside not a soul stirred and the tiny flakes dropped silently. Only the flames of the fire flickered in their syncopated rhythms, and their shadows played in the twilight of the room, making shapes around the walls and in the corners, behind the dancing tongues in the fireplace.

Alice felt nothing but confusion, but the disorientation turned suddenly to alarm as the sound of footsteps echoed outside in the corridor. She sat down on the couch, fluffing up her hair.

Edward sank quickly into an armchair and for a few gaping seconds the room seemed to spin as if it existed independently of the two young figures that had frozen at its different sides. He was straightening his tie when someone called out from the hallway. Grandfather was calling to Rose, who must have arrived to prepare supper, at which the housekeeper cried 'Just a minute!'. Alice held her hand to her mouth to hide her smile, and no one entered. After the steps faded again, Edward stood, walked over and perched beside her, but she moved off.

'Where are you going?' he gasped.

As she disappeared through the doorway Rose could be heard calling out again, but this time Edward was not to be deterred. Just as Alice returned, he took hold of her, capturing her hand. He pulled her up toward him and held her. Alice, incapable of defending herself, moulded her form to him and in the heady glow of the flickering flames their bodies melted together, consumed by a compulsion that was new to both of them.

Chapter 6

Along the cobbled streets of Earl's Court the wind waged its icy onslaught, striking the windows and doors, where the drifts lay in waves. On the carpeted pavements small rows of footprints had impressed themselves. The glittering November morning echoed with the laughter of children dragging sledges, and in the sky church bells peeled, bouncing in the cracks between gables.

Marigold Sanderson, a thick purple stole wrapped tightly around her shoulders, trod tentatively around the corner towards her son's apartment. It was not too far from Hammersmith where she lived, so she could pop in whenever she liked, and she was in the habit of visiting while he was out at work – to tidy up.

She arrived at the doorway and climbed the staircase, shaking the snow from her patent-leather slippers. She let herself in.

'I just don't understand him,' she muttered, picking up the half-empty cup of tea betwixt thumb and forefinger, and pushing about the papers on the desk into a different arrangement.

Of course, she would say nothing to her husband. He would only complain she was mollycoddling.

She polished the Enzo Barbieri violin until the body shone and the pegs and chin rest gleamed. Then she walked into the kitchen and began rattling around among the crockery, her fingers scented with the beeswax.

'That boy needs a good talking to,' she mumbled, as with her clenched fist she banged the tap that objected severely to being turned, coughing and spluttering a miserable spurt of tepid water. She banged it again for good measure.

In reality it was herself that she was annoyed with. Edward's shortcomings when it came to the matter of practice were only to be expected, but his failings when it came to that of choosing a bride were unforgivable. He was just as blind to the reality as his father had been – until she had rescued him.

'Flora is perfect for him,' she continued out loud, abandoning the washing up, and alighting instead on the wooden broom propped up against the iron stove. 'Her father is a bishop. The entire family moves in all the right circles, and they have political connections. Her uncle is the Member of Parliament for Cardiff. If only Edward would see sense.'

She clutched the broom handle even more tightly, sweeping in furious, agitated strokes, and driving the dust into a small pyramid with affection. Her thoughts turned to Mary Brooke and, with a light flick, she swept the pile into the dustpan then, moving into the bedroom, whisked away the pillows and swept the crumbs from the sheet with her cupped hand.

'Dear God, he is as bad as his father,' she muttered on, recalling her son as a small boy who refused to put on the mustard costume with the gold buttons. Even then he had his own ideas, which almost always, in her opinion, were wrong. And the way he spoke to her, without any respect or consideration. Steven, her nephew, and none of the other children treated her so ungratefully. Even when it came to choosing an apartment he had been tricky. How much easier it would have been if he lived at home.

She leaned over Edward's bed, expertly folding his pyjamas and puffing up the pillows that smelled of him. She walked over to the window, and through the icicles that formed intricate crystal ferns on the glass she spotted someone she knew.

Down below a bearded gentleman in a duffel coat was doing his best to balance on a slippery slope, arms up like wings, his right hand clasping a small white bottle that blended with the pavement.

She opened the window a little, and a biting wedge of freezing air howled in. 'Good morning, Mr Jarvis!'

A little shakily, widening his feet to steady himself, Mr Jarvis the milkman looked up nervously, smiled and waved back with his free hand, somehow managing against all odds not to drop the glass milk bottle clenched in the other.

Marigold knew all the local shopkeepers and made it her business to do so. Every day she would visit Johannes at the bakery in Lombard Terrace and pick up all the latest gossip from Arthur when buying her groceries; Mr Jacks the plumber, with his bushy moustache and awkward gait, would always stop to say hello; and if her basket was too heavy, young Peter would always drop his cloths and shoe polish to carry it for her.

Fate had accorded her a modest lot, but at least with Mr Asquith as Prime Minister, the country was in safe hands, and, according to the papers India did not wish to become independent. She needed a holiday. Everyone was off to exotic places these days.

With a cheerful nod she closed the window and Mr Jarvis resumed his earnest negotiation of the pathway. It was at that moment that she decided to attend to the small wicker wastepaper basket, which she couldn't help noticing was full to the brim.

Carefully piecing together the jigsaw fragments of correspondence card, she felt no qualms, for Edward's business was her own, and this applied to all matters. Immediately those three short words, written in Edward's undeniably elegant copperplate hand, danced relentlessly before her eyes: 'I love you'. Turning immediately to the detail of the note, and in particular to the name to which the offending words were addressed, a sudden flutter came over her heart. All of a fluster, she sat down in Edward's chair.

It was Mary she felt sorry for most. Poor Mary had such high hopes of marrying Edward, who knew what she would do if she found out. Indeed, the entire family would be devastated. Forlornly she watched the snowflakes tumble outside the window, musing of the future as if it were a detour, a great, winding, meandering wrong turning with awkward rises and treacherous valleys. It would take strength and persistence, but in the full course of time, Edward would come to his senses.

The snow melted and turned to slush, and the afternoons grew gloomy. Another corpulent, well-intentioned older lady was pre-occupied with her own persistent interrogations, and a trip to the West End theatre was a cunning opportunity to extract the information she was seeking.

'Well?' During the interval over tea Helga Coberg studied the face of her young ward in all its charming detail. 'What have you to tell me?' She replaced the cup on the porcelain saucer and bit into a slice of shortbread.

Alice gave nothing away. 'He visits, it is true, but I'm not sure…'

Helga, who had been regularly bumping into Edward

on the communal staircase at the mansion block for some days, was having none of it. She placed her cup on to the saucer and gazed hard into Alice's eyes.

Alice felt the heat scorching on her pinking cheeks. She had pressed Evie's confidences to her heart like a guilty treasure, dark and intangible; but now Alice had her own secret, and she was not going to tell it.

Helga frowned. 'Does your grandfather know about this... friendship?'

'What friendship?' replied Alice quietly, since Grandfather was working in the library with the door ajar, and she was at pains not to let him hear.

Helga, fond as she was of Alice, was feeling slightly sick. After all, Alice was still a child, and as up and down as the hills and valleys of the Highlands when it came to men. Her marriage prospects were in theory excellent. She had many accomplishments and the world at her feet. As her self-appointed protector, Helga felt she had not only a right but a duty to warn the young, pretty, naïve *ingénue* sitting before her. The world, after all, was a very dangerous place.

Alice glanced towards the window as if innocent of the crime of which she was accused, although she found it hard to define exactly what that was. A low tide of rebellion began to swell within her. If only Evie was here to defend her, but she was not.

She heard herself saying, 'I am sure grandfather and I shall discuss the matter very soon. You needn't worry yourself about it.'

With that she stood up. Smiling politely, she accompanied the lady who wished to act like a mother to her to the second act, vowing not to speak to her grandfather that evening at all about the matter. Only later, after she had returned home, did she remember the letter in her pocket that Rose had brought her earlier. It was from Evie. After reading the words, Alice's fingers released the cartridge paper, and her eyes flooded with tears. Evie had gone to live with her lover, and that all the happy hours they had spent together were behind them.

Chapter 7

Harry had broken with Kitty Smith, but Edward was unaware of the circumstances since Harry had said very little. Whenever one of them felt low they went to the Kings Head. There you could get a large bowl of chicken soup for half a sixpence and as much bread as you could eat and when the basket was empty the waiter brought another.

Harry put down his pint and with a long sigh and no explanation, had delivered the news in a single sentence. He moved on without hesitation to how well his shares were doing in the New Brighton Tower, changing the subject of Kitty as cursorily as if discarding a pair of old shoes.

'Never mind women. There's money to be made in aluminium,' he said, his mouth full of creamed egg. 'China and Japan are mad for it, and even Russia.'

However hard he tried to pretend, Edward was under no illusion of the reality of Harry's emotional state. His bloodshot eyes and unshaven face gave him away.

'Don't worry about me. I'll be fine. I'm not sure she will. All for the best, I'm sure…' he said. 'There are much prettier girls, and much nicer ones.'

Edward shot him a wink, but it was forced. He was enjoying his own romance and his reaction was weak. He was also preoccupied with the problem of parental disapproval and, in particular, his father's expectations.

'What does he actually object to?' asked Harry.

'Everything,' said Edward.

Harry sipped at his Boddingtons and forced a laugh.

They parted soon after, Edward at a loss how to console his friend, since he had not disclosed it, and Harry certain that Edward had not believed a word he had been saying.

That very week the inevitable paternal one-to-one had been arranged and as Saturday approached, Edward found himself at the Reform Club, sitting in one of the bottle-green leather Chesterfield chairs in the library,

Father sat opposite. 'Well, what is all this nonsense?' he said. He lit his pipe and puffed. His manner was genial, and not in any way intimidating. He ordered coffee.

The cautious and more experienced man made no secret of the fact that he had been collecting references from the appropriate sources to determine if Alice would make a suitable daughter-in-law, or that he had consulted a range of sources in order to appraise himself of Alice's background. That meant, on both counts, he had spoken to Edward's mother, but he still lacked some vital facts.

Edward dutifully surrendered the information that was so cheerfully demanded of him and, having heard it, his father settled back into his chair. He was interested to hear that Alice was Scottish and could not help surmising that if there was a war, it might be a blessing to have connections as far away as possible from any danger. Scotland was the safest place he could think of.

Later, steering past the legions of uniformed nannies pushing prams and feeding geese with their charges in St James's Park, Edward pushed up his umbrella with a spring in his step, having won over at least one parent. Mist floated in the red and russet trees, but the weather could not deter him from his next goal. He wound his way to Chelsea undeterred by the rain and the fog shrouding the tower of the South Kensington Museum, which loomed eerily over the freshly painted facades and elegant colonnades.

At exactly five-thirty, Edward took his place behind the desk in another library for his second interview of the day, this time at Carlisle Mansions and to the best of his abilities he answered the very similar series of questions put by his prospective grandfather-in-law.

William Purefoy arrived immediately at the point. 'What is your salary?' he asked Edward. Having heard the figure that only slightly disappointed him, William offered frankly and equally pleasantly the amount of his stipend and the precise details of Alice's trust fund from her parents, a sum that was much higher than Edward had been led to believe by his intended. The interrogation continued through the usual range of topics, spanning unrealistic ambition to unbridled reality until at last, with a cordial handshake, the contract seemed to be secured.

His mother showed none of the reservations she felt in private, but became positively dewy when Edward delivered to her the words that he had so carefully rehearsed in his head. She listened to them carefully, head slightly to one side, hand clasped to her chest, painting Alice in her imagination from her son's glowing description, while secretly comparing her to Flora Nash.

Although she dared not mention to her son that she regarded the Scots as hirsute, loud and without morals, when hearing that Alice had grown up without a mother that her froideur ceased a little.

In due course the meeting between Marigold and Alice went rather better than expected. Alice, keen to impress, surveyed her future mother-in-law with innocent curiosity, and Marigold soon forgot Flora Nash's mother's dinner invitations. On New Year's Eve, together with the Cobergs in their apartment, they all observed the complete Sagitta constellation for the first time, a clear, bright arrow fired, according to legend, at Hercules that just missed him.

Now that they were officially a couple, they could dispense with the stolen kisses, and hold hands when they wanted. A freedom borne of approval meant that they could spend as much time alone together as they wanted, without the interfering glare of a chaperone. They were able to take full advantage of this situation, for hours tasting each other, intoxicated by each other, hardly speaking a word. When at dinner or supper parties with others, they would exchange glances that only they understood.

Winter passed and, as the crocuses pushed up from the tidy grass of Kensington Gardens, Alice often went there to think, sitting on a rug and eating an apple in the sunshine, watching like a child as the clouds skimmed softly above the rooftops of the West End. Her body felt weightless, as she bathed in the sky's warmth, eyes half-closed, hair caressed by the warm breeze.

She recalled the impending gloom in the morning newspapers and promptly dismissed it, seeking refuge in happier thoughts, of Easter eggs she planned to decorate and the French lace she would buy for her wedding outfit. Disjointed images flooded her mind – a butterfly made out of pink icing, the draft of Grandfather's speech, and in the heady mix of planning her perfect future an article she had read about the Tsar faded into insignificance.

Sometimes Edward would go with her and they often bumped into someone they knew. Edward was intrigued and amazed to see what a wide circle of friends and relatives Alice had, although he was saddened to hear of Evangeline's departure. Why Evie did not try to telephone remained unclear. Not even the Professor and Helga, or their nephew Hugh had heard a word from her. No one knew were she was living or what she was doing and it appeared she wanted it that way.

The young couple walked, arm-in-arm, as if it were hard to bear the giddy burden of joy lifting their hearts. The buildings, once grey and desolate, seemed resplendent in the great, hope-filled radiance of the new spring. In the rubbish heaps shards of light dazzled from shattered fragments of glass.

Edward loved Alice's mischievous, reproachful smile, and longed to rest his head on her innocent bosom, but what disappointed reproaches he would have made against her if she had weakened in her resolve against him, for it would only have confirmed his view of the frailty of women who allowed themselves to be seduced in the tempest of a hot-blooded encounter.

He felt almost gratitude towards her for holding back, which made him crave her all the more and knowing this did nothing to dampen his resolve. When alone they found their bodies strained against each other like enemies. In the blazing crescendo of hot breathing and bird's-nest hair and undone clothes it was impossible to tell whether passion or shame would triumph.

Alice, torn between terror and excitement, yielded helplessly before, summoning all her strength, arching her back and stiffening her muscles with a single effort, she managed to release herself. Afterwards Edward would be so cross with her that he would gladly have called off the entire engagement, but the unrelenting sense of wanting to conquer her gave rise to anger at himself for so unfairly putting her into such a compromising situation.

Chapter 8

Beams of light filtered through the upper part of the casement, and as they fell, they became softer and more translucent, as if chiming with the stillness. An owl hooted somewhere outside.

Lost in thought, sitting in the armchair by the window, Edward listened to the languid song, wondering how life could have possibly changed so much in so little time. Only that morning he had tried to pass the German Embassy, but a crowd had gathered outside the building to scream insults. In the resulting riot he had lost his hat.

His bachelor days felt long gone. Moving into Carlisle Mansions had brought its inevitable ups and downs and it was odd to share a home with Alice's grandfather, however genial and polite. Two months of married life had somehow managed to slip by with minor quarrels stemming from insignificant matters, but now the world had fallen into chaos.

In retrospect, it was hardly surprising that Alice had reacted so negatively when he had returned from the Whitehall Enlisting Office that morning, but surely it was his duty to do what he could to help. He wanted to play his own small part in what was happening. He longed to defend his country and make his family proud of him. And almost every single man in his acquaintance had joined Kitchener's Army. Harry was in training in Battersea and Hugh, who was just sixteen, had managed to get into the

Royal Flying Corp, much to the dismay of his Aunt Helga.

He contemplated his wife as she lay sleeping, filled with relief that the argument was over and that Alice, realizing that there was nothing she could do or say to change his mind, had reluctantly accepted his decision, which surely proved if anything that he had been right. They were meant for each other.

He could smell her sweet, intoxicating scent. She appeared more beautiful than ever. She wore no nightgown as usual, and her uncovered body lay stretched with feline ease. Her flowing tresses spread thick upon the pillow, one arm behind her head. Occasionally a hand moved slightly, reaching for something known only to the world of her dreaming. Her mouth, slightly open, seemed to lift at the corners. She had none of the coquetry he despised in other women, but there was something else. A feeling of possession had given him an acute sense of satisfaction. Alice was his, and only his, and this fact alone awarded her a purity, so that the more unrestrainedly she gave herself to him, the lovelier she appeared in his eyes.

Attempting to distract himself once again from the disquieting images that lingered in his head from earlier that day, he allowed his imagination to wander. He saw the future ahead of them without any war in the world, contemplating what role Alice would play, without once considering she would want to do anything but be a mother to his children and continue with her music.

He could see the tiny clasping hand of a child and its greedy pursed lips beaded with milk against her breast; and his heart opened like a flower. His mind raced on. Now he saw not just one, but two small and beautiful children, both smartly dressed in outfits that in every ribbon and button confirmed Alice's exquisite taste. The little boy would be named James; his sister would be Grace. They would both learn musical instruments. James would be a talented pianist and Grace, a cherubic girl with gold ringlets, would play the harp like her mother. Both children would have the same fine features and wide innocent eyes of their mother, whose face he would be able to see plainly in their every smile.

It was easy to allow herself to be intoxicated by that dream. His muscles began to relax and a warm, honeydew reassurance flooded him. The anxiety that had filled his soul previously dissipated. In his reverie he began to construct a soft, feathery nest of their future together, a beautiful home that resounded with music and laughter.

He wanted to wrap her in the blanket of his adoration. He wanted to shield her and hide her from the ills of the world. He watched, transfixed, unable to believe he had won this beautiful, extraordinary goddess. Nothing in the universe would steal her from him – not even war.

Chapter 9

'Alice!' Edward called up impatiently from the street. His starched collar and wool waistcoat was gone. His hair was shorn and he was wearing his uniform. Without waiting for a response, he tore into the lobby and flew up the stairs, narrowly missing a mother and her small child, which he almost knocked over as he rushed past.

That morning the chit he had been expecting had finally arrived. The entire ninth regiment was leaving immediately.

His kitbag was ready and he had washed and shaved. There was just enough time to say his goodbyes. That was the hard part. A short telephone call to his parents, filled with apologies, met with consternation from his father, although his mother accepted the news with surprising and commendable tolerance.

Now, still fumbling for the key ring in his pocket, he pressed the bell. The door opened and Rose regarded him uncertainly, though she had seen him in uniform several times and his haircut was not new.

'Is my wife at home?' he said, catching his breath.

'She is downstairs,' replied Rose, pointing to the Coberg apartment.

'Please fetch her immediately.'

Edward entered the smoky library where Alice's grandfather was working. The two men embraced, and Edward explained the situation.

William took off his spectacles, and the lines of his brow carved into deep, anxiety-filled grooves.

'Will you say goodbye to the Professor for me?'

William sat down again at his desk, staring into the space. With the creak of the chair and the sound of a palm upon back, the two men began their farewells, and as the handshake became a formal, gentlemanly hug, a worried Alice rushed in. 'How long can you stay?' she gasped.

'Not long.'

She stared at him uncomprehendingly, in denial at the enormity of what was happening. 'And when will you return?'

Edward looked away, because there was no answer he could offer her, but then his eyes returned to hers and said it all.

Tearing herself from their locked gaze, Alice walked out of the dining room. Edward followed her into the bedroom, watching as she knelt before the mahogany chest, her graceful body in an L shape as she rummaged through the contents.

In those few seconds Edward captured her image in his mind and sealed it, like a painting that would hold everything they had ever shared together. He inhaled her delicate, lily of the valley scent, and he hid the memory somewhere safe inside himself; he could not tell exactly where that place was, but it was in the location of his heart, and on a familiar pedestal, along with the laughter, the music and the piercing warmth of her body.

After that he treasured the shapes in the room that had become so familiar to him. He savoured each one, so that all of them would become stamped indelibly on his memory. At last he picked up his violin and followed the smooth neck with his index finger, before replacing it in the velvet of its case. One day, by the grace of a God he did not yet know, he would play it again.

Alice had unearthed the object that had been evading her. It lay now in her palm, a small, round red velvet box out of which she drew a gold locket, carved with a smiling angel. Edward knew that it had been a christening present and that it contained a few strands of her fine, gold curls.

'For luck,' she whispered, her white hand trembling as she extended it to him. He took her in his arms and both of them filled with hot, irrepressible tears. She was shaking, propped up by his chest, the object of an unspeakable, unidentified fear. Edward, struggling with his own over-powering emotion tilted his head backward, but his cheeks were still wet.

'I shan't lose it,' he whispered, smiling over her. She tasted salty and sweet, her damp eyes closed against the murky terror of what the future might hold. His, through their watery sheen, had glimpsed something else as they blinked; not only the shadowy horror that hung over them, but a recollection of white. It was the day when snow had been falling, and their first kiss.

Alice slipped the necklace into his pocket and he felt that mouth yield to him again, this time in torment.

Like a fierce tyrant the clock on the mantelpiece struck five. Their clasp, even tighter now, felt impermeable.

Edward gently released his arms, as if holding porcelain, and Alice's fragile hands dropped from his shoulders. She could not look at him.

Summoning the few ounces of courage he could, he opened the door.

'I'm coming with you…' He turned and there, standing before him, in hat, gloves and raincoat, was Alice.

Rose, too, had appeared from nowhere and was looking

upset beside the hat stand. She dabbed her eyes with her crumpled apron.

But Edward was already through the door. He did not look back as he ran down the stairs. Pausing in the street, he glanced up at the building and was rewarded with a cluster of small hands waving from one of the windows. He picked up his bag and carried on.

Alice followed and caught up with him.

The motorbus was cramped, but amid the stifling odour of sweaty uniforms their hands somehow found each other. Through her raincoat Edward could feel Alice's body, crushed so tightly against his. Neither of them noticed the other squeezed equally oppressively against them. Alice's silky hair brushed his mouth, and momentarily he caught its gentle soap scent.

The flags and banners that had welcomed the French Prime Minister on his visit just a few months earlier had disappeared from Belgrave Road. Instead, soldiers merged with their civilian relatives in the confused dissonance of departures.

Edward and Alice wound their way through the maze, fingers interlocked.

'I'll write every day,' said Alice as they came to the carriage door.

'Me too,' said Edward.

'Aren't you scared?'

'I have you…'

The whistles sounded, their high notes piercing the air in a shrill swansong.

Edward took Alice into his arms and they converged together, seared by their love, their separation only forced when the doors of the carriages began to bang shut one after the other. Then Edward jumped on.

Groaning with its great burden, the train drew off, and Alice held out her hand, walking alongside him as she offered tenderly the tips of her fingers, but as the train gathered speed the intertwined fingers broke away from each other and the hands, held high gradually grew apart.

The wheels clattered, as if the very ground beneath them was shattering, though Alice heard nothing but silence and saw only the fluttering of Edward's green hand-kerchief until the black hole swallowed it.

Edward watched the figure on the platform, now moving, now stiller, smaller, and finally indistinct.

After he had gone Alice stood on the platform, hands frozen, in blank hopelessness, staring at the hole where the train had been. Now there was nothing left other than the hollow distance and the blue moonlight striking the cold, empty rails. The profound shock of Edward's departure left her as helpless and bewildered as an abandoned child left on the faraway shore of some unreachable island.

She watched the emptiness, seeing nothing beyond the impressions of her struggling thoughts. She wanted to help and she wanted to be brave, but she did not know exactly how. Later, when she arrived back home and was chopping vegetables, no music on earth could have consoled her. Although she had much to learn, in her heart she knew that those youthful days of comfort and unflustered peace of mind were over, and that nothing would be the same ever again.

PART II

1915–1916

Chapter 1

A sharp chill whistled through the gaps and chinks in the stone barn. Fully dressed and huddling in his overcoat, Private Sanderson sat up, eyes stinging, face creased and crumpled with sleep. He pulled on the boots that had served him as a pillow, and tried to think. He had marched twelve miles that day, but he remembered none of the roads or the names of villages and towns he had passed.

They had been on the move for three days. Today was Friday, and had said goodbye to Alice on Monday. In his mind's eye he pictured her exactly, in her turquoise coat and hat with the peacock feathers, waving her white handkerchief. He had remained standing for a long time at the carriage end, holding on to the door, unable to turn his back on all that he was leaving. Out of the window he could still just make her out, a blue dot beside the tracks, her flickering silhouette fading before at last it vanished.

Inside the dim carriage the collection of men sat cramped together, occupied by their thoughts. They were a mixed bunch, mostly undersized, their large packs and rifles scattered among them. Some would come back. Some would not. Which group was his?

Apart and alone, Edward leaned his forehead against the cool pane and gazed into the darkness, inhaling the perfume lingering on his collar. Seized by regret, he felt gripped by the urge to rip the door open, jump off on to the invisible rubble and run back. He was recalling his wedding night, treasuring that moment, wrapping it in his memory tenderly, as if it were a jewel to be locked away in case someone might steal it.

He was about to turn the handle when a hoarse voice behind him piped up: 'If you please, sir, would you like a cigarette?'

It was Private Peter Lang, who he had met while training in Battersea Park. Lang must have been twice Edward's age, with a thick mop of unruly grey hair and a weathered, world-weary face. Lang held the match, while Edward grasped the cigarette jerkily between two fingers.

'What do you do?' Edward asked, absent-mindedly, as the train rattled on, gathering speed. He blew a plume of thin white smoke into the darkness.

'I teach mathematics – in Barnes.'

'Are you married?'

Lang nodded. 'Two young children.'

'And do they like mathematics?

'They loathe it!'

Both men laughed.

As he stood there, a little unsteady on his feet, Lang turned from time to time, and stared into the tunnel's abyss.

'And you?'

'Yes,' replied Edward. 'But no children.'

'Yet,' said Lang cheerfully, as if a brave new world was around the corner in which everything would be fine, rather than the uncertain, fearful one that they were travelling towards.

The train emerged from the tunnel and Lang found a seat and closed his eyes. Edward was left with his thoughts once again, as the vibrations of the trains rattled his bones. Outside, at least, there was peace in the fields and woods of England, where nature knew nothing of war. Through the window he watched fruit trees dancing in the sunlight. This green and lovely world was a refuge, and though the very light seemed at times an insult, the mere certainty that beauty persisted somehow offered hope.

They reached Folkestone, all of them, thought Edward, in a somewhat confused daze, smiling blearily at the equally bewildered crowd who waved flags and cheered around the jetty. He had not seen the sea for more than a year. Crossing it might have tricked him into thinking he was on a summer holiday, save for starboard there was a small destroyer – their escort, he assumed.

Already homesick, after lunching at the Chat Noir at Etaples, he had drifted about town waiting for the train that was to take him to his battalion. He had lost Lang on the boat. Perhaps he might bump into his old friend Harry, or someone else he knew, but there was no sign of Private Lloyd, who had come over two weeks ago, and there was no train waiting to take Edward or any of the men on to their next destination. They were expected to walk.

Having rested at the farm for several hours, Edward snapped out of his reveries, and he and his fellows marched on. There must have been several hundred of them in all, an assortment of chaps belonging to three regiments. They had been directed to a training camp located at Armentières. Conversing at the first halt it appeared they had come from all directions. Some were too young to shave, and had yet to begin fighting; others – much older – had come from Gallipoli or Egypt.

Soon they were out of Balancourt, heading for the small hamlet of Fiers, about seven miles south-west of Lille, and Edward was at the front. 'Left, right! Left, right!' They halted regularly every hour, then fell out by the roadside to rest. No drinking was allowed except by order.

Almost all the land in the area had been taken over by the army's detritus, but corn was ripening, and between stems poppies made red splashes. Peasants worked on the land, and the sound of ploughing was a balm. Those who worked did not raise their eyes.

'I want to go home.' The men whistled and sang to keep their spirits up, but there was no band to accompany them or even a solitary fiddle as they called at a signaller's cabin to ask which huts their regiments occupied.

Edward had imagined a civilized introduction to his regiment. He was sure that there would be a meeting with the adjutant who would take down notes before, with due ceremony, he would be introduced to the Colonel who with a firm handshake would welcome him and wish him good luck; but when in the pitch black of night a boy on a horse barked instructions in a thick Swansea twang to a farmhouse beyond a midden accessed via dung heaps, his illusions were shattered.

The cold barn contained little other furniture than two wood bedsteads and two camp beds strewn with bedding and equipment. The floor was littered with un-emptied chamber pots, tins of dirty shaving water, unwashed glasses and half-empty whisky bottles. Loud snores emanated from of the unmade beds where, fully dressed and still in his boots, a soldier was sleeping.

Perspiring and achy, Edward moved over to a space on the red-tiled floor, and by the light of a candle unrolled his blanket. He wondered if the soldier asleep might be his sergeant, then disregarded the thought. If he had been, he would have been awake to meet them.

Still unnerved by the long journey and the events of the last few days, through the slightly ajar door he could make out the lurid glare of a distant church fire, its spire inky against the glow of the sky. A gramophone played something from *The Maid of the Mountains*. It reminded him of one of Frederick Coberg's summer reviews. Suddenly he was transported to the Art's Club garden and the scent of Alfred Carrière roses drifted in his nostrils. Turning over on his side, Edward thought he smelt Alice's perfume, before exhaustion took over, launching him into the realm of a fitful slumber.

He woke with a jolt and the deafening blast of a bugle. Muzzy and fog-headed, he could hear someone shouting from the next room that it was time to get up.

The sergeant who shouted the order, Eustace Talbot, was the soldier who had been sleeping when Edward had arrived. A tall thin man with a hooked nose and a slight stoop, he wore the DCM, but his manner was casual, although his keen, intelligent eyes were unusually bright. As he stepped away, Lang confided to Edward that he had heard Talbot was the bravest man in the regiment, who obtained his medal by saving fifteen privates, single-handed, the previous winter.

The Bull Ring was a great open plain where several hundred men were put through their paces by sergeant majors seemingly selected on account of their shrill voices and austere manner. For five days the men climbed among its sand dunes and practised firing grenades and throwing Mills bombs.

Every minute of every hour was taken up by training. Drill 9-10; bayonet skills 10.15-11.15; lecture on pay and mess book 11.30-12.30; fitness 2-6.30. In the bare field they cultivated ferocity before sacks, and learned the most ungentlemanly ways of dispatching their enemies before listening to a lecture by an elderly officer on the virtues of the bayonet. They learned about gas, tried putting on the clammy flannel bags otherwise known as PH helmets and ran obstacle races on a prepared course. Every afternoon they returned, hot and exhausted, to the farm to eat bully beef and bread.

Despite the exhausting schedule, Edward felt curiously optimistic. They had been training on this hillside at X in the baking heat for five days, and bathing in the river below, and they were a little more measured. So far he had managed not to injure himself or any of his fellow soldiers and although he was unfit he was becoming stronger. There was no more dashing hell-for-leather, screaming, like children playing Red Indians.

Already there were two letters from his mother, one with the news that his father, being considered too old too enlist for active duty, had taken on a senior position at the War Office. He had received three brightly coloured silk-sewn cards from Alice, all conveying the same cheery messages about a new harp piece she was learning by Salzedo. Everyone was well and the two families were looking forward to his return soon.

Tingles of joy combined with guilt as he read the letters and vowed to write back, but he didn't have time to send long responses. He was too busy getting to know the men of his platoon. About half of them were miners, short, stocky, steady men, used to hard work and not given to grousing. Nelson, with the quiet voice of a poet, was a bachelor and by religion a Catholic. Talbot stood next to him on parade. He was the platoon Hercules, a hard drinker with the stomach of an ox who would box anyone in the regiment for fun.

The trades of the rest made a motley list: labourer, farmer, carpenter, painter, blacksmith. Stone, a wisp of a man, who had been to India with the regular army, was something of a puzzle. He was smart enough, but seemed distracted and unresponsive.

The spirits of the company were greatly improved by the general cheerfulness of a northerner named Porter, a tight, brisk little man with pocked cheeks. He had the air of an old bachelor who stood no nonsense and with the habit of speaking his mind.

Fitzroy, an older man with a nose was shaped like the bill of a parrot, and heavy, knitted eyebrows, seemed the most awake of the privates. Edward did not know what to make of him, with his cold, vague, wary eyes. He had served in Gallipoli, but they did not know his record.

On Saturday evening too many men crowded into a small room, each saluting as he came before a grey-haired, red-faced Welshman who sat writing at a table. Standing by his side was a short, raw-boned and with a dour look. He was their medical officer.

They were determined to like the new colonel despite his untrustworthy eyes and weak voice; and everyone was glad the old one had gone. Other new officers had arrived, among them Jessop who had taken over number nine platoon of the company. He appeared an excellent fellow, without any frills.

The Colonel put on a cheerful expression. He had not seen Ypres. He just sent others there. His chief interest appeared to be in taking prisoners. 'Shoot the bastards. Alternatively, if you bring them in I'll shoot them, and I might shoot you while I'm at it', was the way he put it.

After the short lecture they saluted and filed out. What had this man done except disillusion them? Edward thought to himself, seething silently. They all knew the odds. Most had been with the battalion for just a few days. They were volunteers and their prospects of survival the worst in memory. Nerves bristling, the men sat around on their camp beds, while Talbot delivered his own brand of speech.

He was a coarse-fibred creature. His hair, prematurely grey, was thinning; his complexion ashen and the twinkle still visible in his eye, was fading. He was a blend of order and chaos, with a keen sense of duty and simultaneously a rejection of authority.

He smiled wryly. He had seen what it was like. 'You'll be dead in a week,' he said first off, 'all of you. You're in for the lot. Where's that whisky? You'll need whisky when you get into those trenches.'

Any awkwardness at the silence that followed soon gave way towards cheerful affability, and a warm glow of optimism pervaded the room. Soon the crowd seemed abandoned to fate, and Nelson and Stone, who were not usually given to gambling, were playing cards.

Edward drank to his new chums with a heavy sigh. There were many bottles on the table, and the cigarette smoke wafted with his memories. The image of William Purefoy's kind face as he had once toasted life would not leave him. He reached for the bottle and poured. 'This war will be won on whisky!' he shrugged, to which each man responded with a loud cheer.

Outside it was raining, but as soon as the sun appeared it dried the damp mud. Long before then the men had received their orders. A chit from the orderly room had come to Talbot at midnight, and when he read the fairly mundane-sounding words – 'Companies will dig a new communication trench' – aloud they were a tad slurred.

Before it was light, belts had been cleaned and tin helmets found. The sergeant had reported all present and correct, and by eight o'clock sharp that evening they had begun marching, even though no man felt ready as, descending the long hill leading to Dickebush, they dodged the flow of trucks and ambulances that stirred and spattered the dirt into mounds.

From his position ten or twelve back in the column, Edward could make out a small Irish regiment as it emerged ahead from the other direction. Each regiment halted and a major came over to greet them. Word trickled down the line that there was heavy shelling on the trench they were bound for. The battalion had had a terrible time in Sanctuary Wood. It did not bode well.

The Menin road, which ran east and a little south from Ypres, was like a vein from the bleeding artery of the Front. Ambulances, horses foot soldiers and bicycles careered along this road. Night and day it brought everything from ammunition and artillery to spam and soup. War had rolled back civilization from the dejected, desolate landscape surrounding the road. Pale shadows chased over the land as the men marched, excited and afraid, following unfamiliar orders they did not fully understand, to meet their destiny.

The platoon was two miles south of Plas when it reached the billet, a large mansion standing in a low valley beneath tall polar trees that seemed to have guarded it for centuries. From a distance the house looked grand, but the men were not exactly guests in French houses and the rooms were all closed up, apart from two bedrooms via the back staircase, only available because French law obliged the owner to give them as accommodation.

The men were informed after their long, exhausting march that their orderlies could not cook in the enormous kitchen but had to make a campfire in a cold, muddy field before they could have a cup of tea; and they were not allowed to use any of the six large lavatories in the house.

Instead the sanitary squad were forced to dig holes over half a mile away.

At sunset Edward climbed the steep, stony slope, the light jangling in his eyes. He could make out the rumble of the guns and see the red, white and blue lights of the planes. Every now and then a German machine would pass the line and there would be a tac-tac-tac of fire and a cloud of smoke. At intervals there was silence, but to his tired, sensitive ears this absence of sound was acute pleasure. He drank it in, trying to make sense of the shapes he saw..

Eastwards, following the purple clouds, gun flashes flickered in a bizarre aurora borealis, to the belching of explosions. From this vantage point it was possible to see the scale of destruction caused by shelling. For miles the countryside had been decimated. On the horizon golden trees stood twisted into forlorn shapes. Down at the other side of the hill lay wire, broken rifles, ammunition, mess tins and equipment littered the chaotic ground. A white skull glistened from the black earth.

Head swirling, feet skidding, he stumbled on the way down. In a heartbeat he became aware of the skin on the tips of the fingers of his left hand as they reached to grip on to something. He drew out the splinter from his palm and watched the blood run. This was no time to be foolish about love. At the same time only love mattered.

Chapter 2

Alice woke to find the blankets in a tangled heap. Pins and needles buzzed in her hands and tiny hairs bristled on her freezing legs. Opening and closing her eyes, she wondered where she was. Everything felt alien. The empty bed was cold and the pillow smooth. A man's trousers lay on the chair. They belonged to Edward and she had left them there, exactly where he had put them,

At the realization that her husband had gone, a fleeting wave of disbelief swept over her. She sat up, glimpsing her white face in the wardrobe mirror. She could still hear the thundering of the Widor on the organ, smell the violets in her bouquet and the smile on Grandfather's luminous, overwhelmed face. It was that day, her wedding day, the 2nd March 1914.

Her head sank down on the pillow, and she sought refuge in easier thoughts. The memory acted like a balm, but it did nothing to dispel the dismay that had crept up on her. Hugh who was stationed near Mormelon-le-Grand, had written three long letters, and Jasper had written twice, but she had received no letters from her husband, only three short postcards, mostly telling her not to worry. All three had come in the first fortnight of his absence. She read between those scrawled, hurried lines something else along with hope. Instinctively, in the bland, almost formulaic accounts of what he had eaten, what time he had risen, how he had slept, indicated something of his own isolation. Attending the lecture by Mrs Ellen Terry and accompanying Helga Coberg to *The Three Musketeers* at the Shaftesbury did nothing to soothe her frayed nerves. Unable to bear the aching silence from Edward, she decided she needed to occupy herself. Kitty Smith was learning to drive ambulances and even Helga had joined the Women's Royal Voluntary Service.

The Second London General Hospital stood on a busy street extending from the public house known as World's End to Fulham and Hammersmith. Two schools formed part of the building and their joint playgrounds made a large area where huts and tents housed the growing number of wounded.

Alice's first patients were the dying plants. Twenty-three pots in the wards needed attention, some porcelain, others brass, and one hanging basket containing ferns. She spent the entire first week caring for them. Each had to be removed and soaked under a tap every day. When the aspidistras did not wilt did she began in earnest and only then, while she was still training, was she allowed to empty bedpans, carry sputum cups and change dressings.

Propelled by some raw, unseen sense of doom, as the relentless winter dragged on, she plunged into duties she had never once in her life imagined that she would be doing. In the cold autumn mornings she left home at six, either taking the motorized omnibus or walking to the hospital. In the ward she and a ragtag and bobtail selection of other girls preparing spent their days dressing trays and supporting limbs using plinths and pulleys. In the evenings she returned home to darn socks and read medical books. Grandfather seemed to rally, thanks to the penicillin administered by the doctor and to Rose's broth, but there was something in her guardian's manner and his persistent stoop that needled at what was left of her security.

Edward's scent still lingered in the apartment – on the scarf he had left on the hat stand, on his suits that hung in the wardrobe and on the handkerchiefs in the chest of drawers. At night the few early notes he had written to her stayed safely tucked beneath the pillow. She knew every sentence.

Winter passed in a bewildering chaos of increased casualties and exhausting shifts. Gradually, Alice memorized all the names of the antiseptics, learned how to tie bandages and slings, and how to syringe boils and by March she was considered sufficiently competent to perform clerical duties such as ordering swabs, splints and bandages and monitoring food supplies. Eventually, although she still had everything to learn about the gulf between the ideal of administering humane care and the practical reality of stomach-churning open wounds, she was allowed to wash patients with carbolic soap.

Since it was always Edward that she was nursing by default, she administered the carbolic soap with a steely determination and professionalism that surprised everyone. Even Matron, a stickler for high hygiene standards, watched with raised eyebrows, having witnessed so many young VADs come to the ward expecting to hold patients' hands and fluff pillows.

Chills and colds resulted from the gloomy, damp days, before fog developed, piling up white and still against the windows. By six o'clock the lampposts outside were invisible and the gentle patter of hurried footsteps on the pavements had grown a little fainter. When the throb and clamour of the ward subsided a little, Alice felt her way down the slippery steps into the blankness, and then to the brittle grass that cracked and crunched under her feet. She knew where she was when the waft of stale beer that emanated from the doorway of the King's Head hit her nostrils.

Whilst Edward's situation remained oblique, every day brought messages announcing new horrors. Sir Archibald drowned when the Lusitania was sunk, and Mr Morley's son had been killed at Mons. Kitty Smith's elder brother had fallen at St Quentin; Mr Morley's son had been blinded at St Eloi; and Rose had lost a cousin at Arras.

To make matters worse, Grandfather's health seemed to be failing, although he did not complain.

Helga Coberg summed up her purgatory later that evening when she came to visit.

'I do fear for you, dear child. You are young and beautiful. You must take care of yourself. Working yourself to death will not bring Edward back. If you continue in this manner, you will serve no one.'

As Alice walked with her to the door, Helga turned to say, 'You really must come out for dinner with the Countess, dear. There will be a large group and some very interesting people. The war should not mean you have to stop living and people are dying doesn't mean you have to give up.'

Slipping down the stairs until out of sight, she called back, 'Don't be late!' and then her front door clicked shut.

Chapter 3

It was not a long march, only ten miles, but on a hot day with several days' marching behind and with forty pounds on his back it merited endurance. They continued in single file around a wide horseshoe bend, stumbling over discarded sandbags and ration packs. It was gone five the following afternoon when they finally arrived at the communication trenches, and by then everyone was exhausted.

Edward was thankful for the water in the petrol can that bore its flavour, but by the stony look on Fitzroy's face he could tell the man was less impressed.

'Pah!' Fitzroy spat out the liquid and threw his mess tin over his shoulder. He wolfed down a biscuit, eyeing Nelson, who was so tired his head had already fallen on to his humped shoulder.

'Have you seen Lang?' Edward said, trying not to look Fitzroy in the eye.

Nelson, who was sitting opposite, propped up against his rifle, shook his head from side to side.

'Is anyone going to get us some tea?' Sergeant Talbot glanced searchingly around the group.

Everyone looked down, except several young lads, one rosy-cheeked and with an almost cherubic face, who looked flustered.

Another man, whose name Edward did not yet know, almost choked on his bully beef. Then someone yelled 'Get your own!'

So much for brotherly camaraderie, thought Edward to himself. At that moment Lang reappeared and made tea, and the group relaxed.

They were in Diependaal, just a little to the left of the trenches the battalion held last year. Fusiliers were on their right flank, another company to their left. The land to the front sloped up for a few yards and then rose again in a long sweep. Just to the right it was possible to discern the tower of the church at Heuvelland, half-hidden by a small copse of withered, torn trees. At the base of the valley broken trucks lay upturned.

As Edward and the others soon discovered, moving along a trench was not easy. For a start it was not straight for more than four yards. In some places there were odd turn-offs to other dugouts, while in others there were steps down and up where a section of parapet had been blown in or walls of a traverse had collapsed.

At first the maze of exits and entrances seemed so intricate that it was hard to tell whether a wrong turning might not lead straight into enemy lines. Engineers were busy on two deep dugouts that would be capable of accommodating half a company, and the Tunnelling Corps was laying a mine. Within the trench men were revetting with wire and sandbags, and laying down new duckboards.

From where Edward was standing, he could see very little of this or anything else that was going on. Glancing around at the endless earth, he wanted to scream. They couldn't possibly be expected to live and sleep here, could they? The entire network seethed with decay and excrement. It had rained for several days and the orange of the trench oozed evil-smelling liquid.

After four hours of digging mud, carrying wire, stakes, rations, bombs and duckboards, he came out of the trench, along with Lang and a few others, for a brief respite to wash and shave before going back in again. There was no time to think of home or to write letters.

The hour and the light ruled trench routine. Unless patrols were out, at night there were three men on duty and two on sentry while the others rested. When the sun rose the sentries remained at their posts, while the others went to sleep or ate breakfast.

At dawn Talbot usually retired to the dugout to write his report, which always included the wind's direction. At around seven the Sergeant sent a couple of men to bring in dixies of hot tea from the field kitchen in the village, and again at twelve and four for lunch, Maconachie mostly, and tea. Mid-morning a dozen or so 5-9 shells usually came over and after that there was almost always quietness until stand-to at sunset.

Rats gibbered and squeaked all over the cast-up earth and everyone wasted a good supply of revolver ammunition potting at them. Twice during the night Edward felt one wriggle beneath his feet and noticed the strip of sacking that served as a ceiling was bulging about. He pulled out his revolver and fired, and the creature fell limp above his head. It struck him that only a month ago he had never seen a rat, and now, here he was, shooting one.

Life had altered beyond recognition. He had exchanged blue skies for dark, sunless mud. It was as if his previous life had not existed. He was prepared for the lack of sleep, but nothing could have prepared him for the hunger. He missed Alice's shepherd's pie.

Five days of hard labour were needed to fully dig out the trench, during which time the sun blazed down on them. Each morning, passing a dump, the men drew a pick or shovel. Why spend so long teaching a man to fire a rifle when he needed only a shovel?

As the tape was laid a dozen whizz-bangs fizzed around them, glaring red as they burst. Each man fell to his knees.

'What the devil are you doing?' screamed a disgusted Talbot. 'Get up!'

By some small mercy no one was hit, but at 1.30 p.m, alarming messages began to come in from Gheluvelt reporting that part of the line was falling. As the order came to withdraw, the entire company worked their way back to an estaminet. That afternoon, on the 7th October 1914, the order arrived to advance. Each man prepared for the worst.

The battalion was deployed along a high ridge that provided excellent cover. Ahead the Germans were pounding the wire-enclosed fields with heavy shellfire, sending deafening waves throughout the entire region. The infantry had advanced and a violent battle continued all along the line of the woods.

Hardly five hundred yards off the German offensive hidden behind Hellfire Corner broke cover. The noise was terrifying, as if the entire sky had collapsed, but no matter how the shellfire rumbled and cracked the enemy remained hidden.

Edward ran, heart hammering against his ribcage, and climbed to the top of the tower. Crouched behind the parapet, he surveyed the German positions through his field glasses.

Shell bursts, one after the other, kept coming. Small green flecks could be seen, retreating in clusters of ten or twenty. Wild rifle fire rang out in all directions and a rain of bullets sang around and above. The machine guns began to rattle and afterwards the shells, reverberating at the sides.

Then there was nothing. The glasses shook in his hands. His skin and nose itched with the dust blowing in the wind. Reaching into his pocket, he drew out the locket Alice had given him when he had left London. What could she be doing now? But this was not the time for answers.

Ahead of him shells began to burst in one of the groups, and small flecks, lifted from the ground as they were cast into the air, dropped to earth, scattering men and horses like confetti. A bee swarm of airplanes appeared gradually, the buzz of their engines rising and falling. Nearer and nearer they flew, until they whirled overhead before retreating into the fading sunlight.

He waited. Three shots rang out, one after the other. That was the signal. Rifle in hand, he was aware of running down the stone steps and into the distance, but where he was going or why he did not know.

How many hours the inferno continued he could not tell, for the minutes and hours merged into a disjointed blur of desperate, deafening fighting. By the end he had four holes in his coat as a souvenir.

As the sky darkened a strange silence extended in every direction and the land, stiff and frozen in the presence of death, lay as if mesmerized. The moon glimmered icy white and the faraway trees seemed to huddle, limpid, under its light. Tiny columns of smoke began to rise above the mud as the men filled their tins with bully beef and powdered chocolate cake.

Edward gazed at the Plough dipping towards the horizon. What sages the stars had become, guardians of a peace beyond human madness that no gun could shoot.

That day the battalion lost two men, and eighteen horses were killed. There was good news as well. A captured order stated that the Kaiser had informed Three

If

Army Corps that Ypres must be taken at all costs.

After they had eaten the mail was handed out. Edward read Alice's two letters by candlelight.

'My beloved: I fear you may not have received my earlier letter, which I wrote the evening you left. Now it is morning and I am unable to stop thinking of you. The Cobergs have been very kind, and Grandfather…'

Edward read on for three long pages. From every line of the sloping handwriting seeped Alice's tearful longing. It occurred to him how young she was. He read on:

'Please write to me, darling. I am so worried for you. I can hardly bear it.'

It was drizzling lightly and the ink mingled with the mud. Through the bitter stench of gunpowder another scent, so faint as to be indiscernible, carried to his nostrils. It was the sweet, delicate fragrance of lily of the valley. He picked up the sodden paper and saw Alice's clearly, the almond eyes and white alabaster skin.

Afterwards, he rifled through the other envelopes and cards, recognizing his mother's handwriting on two of them. With difficulty, on the reverse of a picture of the Notre Dame, he made out Harry Lloyd's almost illegible scrawl. The note indicated that he was alive and well and wished him luck; and he was delighted to open the small parcel tied with brown string. It was from the Cobergs, and it contained a fruit loaf. At last he came to a thin, pale-grey envelope with his name, service number and regiment were scribbled in capital letters. He opened it with a casual curiosity.

'Dear Edward,' it read. 'I hope this message finds somehow finds its way to you. I have reflected long and hard about whether to contact you to inform you that your wife has been seen arm in arm with another man. I cannot divulge the exact details, and it may be an innocent friendship, but I felt that you should know. I know this is a sensitive matter and therefore hope you will forgive me for not disclosing my identity.'

His fingers slipped and the letter fell. It was unsigned and the postmark had been smudged. The wide, almost childish hand was unfamiliar. He racked his brains to think who might have been so bold as to meddle in his personal affairs in this way. One by one, he ran through the guests at the wedding, the mutual friends and tricky relations, but he could think of no one who could have written such an upsetting message, intended no doubt to drive a wedge between a young, happy couple.

Screwing up the paper into a tiny ball, he told himself that it was all nonsense. 'Arm in arm' was not 'hand in hand'. The author of the note had probably witnessed an innocent show of affection with someone Alice had known since childhood. It was a misunderstanding. Either that, or else someone was trying to make mischief.

Seeking reassurance, Edward returned to the letter from Alice:

'My darling, no one understands the impermeable wall that exists between us. It feels unbreakable as steel, as wide as a continent and as high as the moon. I lie down. I wake. I go to bed, overcome by exhaustion. I know you would write to me if you could, but I refuse to believe that you are gone. If you read these words, please know that it is because of my love for you that I am desperate and that I await your safe return. Nothing matters more than you. I know I have no right to complain, I who live in a safe place.'

Edward's shoulders relaxed. There was no cause for alarm. The anonymous meddler was misguided. He knew Alice better than anyone. At the same time, a seed of doubt had been planted. Something needled at him, though he could not say exactly what it was. His mind turned to Jasper Lenz. He recalled him asking Alice to dance at their wedding.

'May God keep you safe, my love. I am always here for you. Your Alice.'

He pressed his nose to the paper and breathed her in one more time. He folded the letter and, with a long sigh, put it into his pocket, and then immediately he wrote his response, omitting any mention of the anonymous note. As soon as he had leave, he would return home to England, where he would discuss it with his wife face to face.

As he was about to turn in, he suddenly remembered the other letter, the one he had been holding on to for Lang, but Lang was still nowhere to be seen.

'Lang!' he cried. He shouted again, louder this time, his hand cupped hand around his mouth, but there was no response. It was another voice that answered his call.

'He's dead,' said someone in a broad Yorkshire accent. It was Geoffrey Porter. He strode off before Edward had a chance to respond.

His hand gripped the paper, fixed and immobile. Surely Lang couldn't have gone already. Still unable to grasp what had happened, he stood there, gazing into the empty, ghost-filled night.

Lang's letter remained in his clenched fist for a long time before, resisting the temptation to read its contents, he came to Lang's inert, waxen face and the body, twisted and limp, exactly where it had fallen below the parapet. Quietly, gently, he slipped the envelope, still unopened, into the chest pocket and pulled the blanket over the torn, lifeless head. He settled down, drifting, until a restless sleep overpowered him.

Chapter 4

Imagine a vast semicircle of lights, a cross between those of the Thames embankment and those of a fleet out at sea. Only, instead of fixed yellow lamps, they are powerful white flares, sailing up every minute and burning for twenty or thirty seconds, before fizzing out like rockets. In between a slim shaft swung around among the stars, hunting an invisible airplane; and every second of it flashed in the sky like the opening of a furnace door. All this was visible miles away, each explosion lighting up every man, tree and bush for at least half a mile.

From the relative safety of the billet, Edward watched, transfixed, as an aeroplane twisted and turned. Notes of charcoal lingered in his nostrils. It tasted like steam and sulphur with a hint of urine from the saltpeter. From somewhere ahead the random rat-a-tat-tat of snipers gave no clue as to the origin of the firing.

It seemed impossible to believe he had survived in this hell for over four months. Just one more week and he would be going home – and it was almost Christmas. Just the thought of it allowed him to dream. In his mind he tried to recapture what it would be like to hold Alice again and as he breathed in the memory of her face he could almost taste her. Try as he might, he could not stop thinking of that anonymous letter. When he was home he would ask her about that dreadful anonymous letter he had received, without accusing her directly, since he did not think her guilty. He would patiently listen while she told him the truth about it. His thoughts turned to his parents and he thought how happy he would be to be surrounded by all those he loved.

By the following day, despite every man's best efforts, the battle along the line of the woods near Lys had intensified. At four o'clock the order everyone had been dreading came through from their commanding officer. The battalion was to advance that night.

As the hour approached, Talbot began rallying the men and passing around rum. Some appeared to be in good spirits, others began to pray. Nelson, rosary in one hand, wrote in his diary with the other. Watson and another lad whistled. Stone put on a brave face and Fitzroy sat silently staring into the darkness, his once crisp, clean uniform now caked in mud.

Edward clutched the locket Alice had given him. 'For you,' he whispered. He kissed it before slipping it into his pocket. Then he scribbled a hurried note to her. He folded it into four and on the outside wrote, 'For Alice, in the event I should not survive.'

When the time came the men crept over the field as hurriedly as possible, so as not to be silhouetted against the light. Even then, each one suspected they had seen their last daylight.

On they hurried, down the zigzag pathway that ran along the hedgerow beside the river, and which was known only to them. The sound of their breathing was loud, the stillness broken only by the croaking of frogs, the crackle of boot upon stick, or the deafening thunder of a heartbeat.

They moved in single file beside the stream, straight

into the wood. Fitzroy went first, then Nelson, after that the rest. Edward brought up the rear with Talbot. Soon they were on their stomachs, wriggling through the patch of long grass for a hundred yards, past the willows, pausing occasionally to listen. Tiny noises seemed too loud – a rat nibbling at corn, a rabbit sitting between the long blades; and now a heavy rustling to the right, near the reeds.

The blue moon lit up the wood in white and brown. From here they could see everything. Over every bush, hedge and every fragment of wall floated a thin film of smoke, betraying a machine-gun. Where on earth were they? Goddammit. They were up in the trees.

Cold sweat broke on the back of Edward's neck. His revolver hammer went back with a click and his hand steadied. A shot rang out and then another. In the confusion that followed one man went down in full flight, but the others kept on moving. Who was firing? He couldn't tell. He was conscious of running forward, of a firework launching in his ears. Then, all at once, the light was extinguished. He was on his back and the fine, filmy clouds were flying silently above him. The thought occurred that he was floating inside them, that his soul had soared up and had become one with them.

That was the last thing he remembered. When he woke up his head was numb and all that was happening around him was like the continuation of a surreal dream. Before him stood two grey-uniformed officers, one casually smoking a cigarette, in his right hand a bayonet, his polished boots and buttons gleaming in the moonlight.

Other men had been disarmed as well. Watson stood, his shoulders slumped, behind him men lay bent in strange positions. An arm poked out from the ground as if still fixed to an unseen, buried body. Blood seeped into a wide, black pool behind a discarded helmet.

Inside the truck it was dark and cramped. Edward sat beneath the tarpaulin roof, dazed from being bludgeoned unconscious on the back of the neck, blinking repeatedly, wondering where he was.

The large blurred image crisped; and his gaze fell upon the soldier sitting opposite him, yawning and extending his arms. He recognized this man. It was Geoffrey Porter, the sergeant who had handed him Lang's letter. Porter's brittle, stubbly face was unmistakable, devoid of all its previous mirth.

Suddenly, the doors swung open. Edward felt himself being pushed forward. Something sharp prodded his back. The cacophony of orders intensified as they were rounded up with bayonets and buttheads and pushed into a train carriage.

The engine chugged into the blackness and into the silent unknown. The wheels clanked and jangled over the interchanges. Then there was nothing.

Edward woke with a jolt. A faint breeze entered the stale air of the carriage from the cracks in the window. The light was pink and growing more luminous as it reflected on the metal. Around them others, who had also been sleeping, began to stir.

To his left someone let out a grating, painful cough, chest rattling with mud and tormented by phlegm. Eventually the lungs, like ancient bellows, settled again. 'Where are we?' wheezed the voice. It belonged to Peter Stone, the blacksmith.

Edward shook his head. Up ahead, a town rose out of the dawn, its Romanesque church spires piercing the limpid sky like spears, but it could have been anywhere.

Stone, his high brow raised, stared at the bleak, stone

buildings; his eyes, with their mauve, shadowy sockets, told of his exhaustion. The small circles around his irises were bright red.

'Is it hell?' Fitzroy sat up straight and leaned towards the glass pane with an expression that was the epitome of dread. He was a father of five children.

Watson, whose chubby, rosy-cheeked face was earnest and curious in its mirrored flection, looked suddenly old. He began biting his nails and as he flicked his fingers through his close-cropped hair he suddenly reminded Edward of Harry Lloyd. Edward wondered if he would ever see his old friend again. The last he heard Harry was at Nanteuil-le-Haudouin.

They were all privates, but Peak was an orderly. He sat motionless, arms folded, absorbed in his own thoughts, as if he too could not believe he had landed in this predicament already, having been fighting for only a few weeks.

'Does anyone know what happened to Captain Talbot? Or Nelson?'

No one answered Edward's question, so he assumed the worst. Hardly another word passed between them, so preoccupied were they with their own angst and desperation.

Only Stone, in his lilting twang, ventured a few disjointed phrases, as he heaved and puffed.

'Do you still have that hip flask?' he croaked. He glanced at Porter.

'Here...' said Porter in his broad Yorkshire accent. He held out his almost-empty water bottle.

The train screeched to a halt and German soldiers in their unmistakable grey uniforms bearing heavy rifles, clustered around the carriage doorways and the captives, wracked by the journey, piled out like mackerel released from a fishing net. Gathering around them on the station platform, the Germans began barking in their guttural, spiky, spitting tongue, wielding their guns and herding the British men like cattle.

There must have been at least a hundred men in all, a pool of khaki surrounded by a grey border. Beyond the mass, swathes of people dressed in civilian clothes were attempting to sell things or to beg for money. Local merchants in thick, long overcoats jostled with farmers wearing spotted cravats and flat caps. The arrival of the captives was an event and a spectacle, but, above all, a chance to make money.

At the gate a swarm of officials began to examine and search them. One, a strapping straw-haired soldier, made it his business to tip out the entire contents of Edward's kit bag and to relieve him of his watch. Fitzroy delved into his pocket, drawing out a packet of Gauloises, which he offered to the German. 'Courtesy of the British army.' Fitzroy's grimace almost resembled a smile.

The Hun looked sheepishly around to check no one was looking. His chiselled, flat face warmed a little, and with a dexterous slip of the wrist the packet was in his pocket. After that the search was perfunctory and some bags he did not even bother opening. Edward was relieved that the knife strapped to his inner right calf went unnoticed.

By noon the inspection was complete and the list drawn up. Everyone was accounted for. Out of Edward's team, only Porter, Stone, Watson and Fitzroy were accounted for. The others must have been killed back in the woods near Lys.

The men lined up and one of the Germans told them in disjointed, twisted English that from now on their fate would be determined by the Kaiser himself.

Outside the station a great crowd had amassed. Women and children stared, their faces fearful and inquisitive, but not hostile. They seemed fascinated to watch at such close quarters the enemy of whom they had heard so much. The prisoners for their part, half-expecting they were marching towards their deaths, stared back, and in this zoo it was impossible to tell who were the animals.

One by one, in single file they marched, through medieval cobbled streets, past quirky shops brimming with knick-knacks and small taverns and cafés where more people turned to peer at them. In the market square they were ordered onto the back of another truck, its brown sides caked in gloopy mud. A painted sign swayed in the wind. He was still in France, in a place named Sedan, although he had never heard of it.

By the time they had arrived at their destination, fortress of barbed wire and expressionless guards, the white sky had faded to grey. Inside the building the large rooms were bare and unheated. Voices lingered on the damp air as if detached from the bodies to which they belonged; words in languages Edward did not understand echoed towards the high metal ceilings. He ate the stale bread and thin, murky cabbage soup put before him, but exchanged few words with the others. Perhaps there would be a firing squad at dawn. Perhaps this was their last supper.

The bunks were hard wooden benches over which filthy blankets had been thrown, but each of them was so weary that their heads fell on the lumpy straw pillows with exhaustion. That was apart from Stone, whose lungs were still troubling him and whose staccato coughing punctuated the regular, low beat of snoring.

Edward, too, lay awake, gazing open-eyed at the

vacuum above, holding Alice's golden locket, relieved to have survived for now. He saw in that emptiness only Alice. He saw her laughing and imagined her playing her harp. Then he remembered the anonymous letter. Gripped by a sudden jealousy, he saw her holding hands with Jasper Lenz. He was consoling her, whispering to her, and seducing her.

'I wonder who's kissing her now, Wonder who's teaching her how; wonder who's looking into her eyes; breathing sighs, telling lies…

Chapter 5

Marigold's eyebrows were raised, her head lowered, as if she were about to burst into tears. She dabbed her eye with her handkerchief and tried not to look flustered. She was extraordinarily pale.

The telegram did not say much. An Officer in charge of the Battalion Records had sent it, although the name was not familiar. It was dated 28th January 1915.

'Madam, I regret to inform you that a report has been received from the British Expeditionary Force. Your husband is missing in action.'

Alice, who had been standing by the mantelpiece, sat down. The thin, filmy paper fell from between her fingers and her heart cracked against the bones of her chest, but it was not what she feared, that gut-twisting news she dreaded the most, that of her husband's death.

'In all likelihood, he is still alive,' said Humphrey, sitting forward in the Chesterfield chair and warming his hands on the fire. If Edward had been killed, he would surely have been the first to know about it. It was at least one advantage of having a job at the War Office.

'I feel sure he is all right,' said Alice. She tried to stay calm. Edward would write soon. She was convinced of it.

As the clock struck five, Marigold tried to change the subject. They chatted about small, irrelevant matters before Marigold turned to Alice. 'So what are you going to do?', she said. There must be something…' She looked hard into

Alice's eyes, as if unable to help feeling that Flora Nash would have had something more impressive to say for herself.

'I'm not sure,' said Alice, who was struggling with her own emotions. She crossed her legs, fidgeting from one position to another. She had no clue how to placate her mother-in-law.

In reality Marigold was smarting. Edward had not sent her even a postcard since he had left last August, yet Mr Jacks had managed to send cards to everybody. Even Mrs Jarvis, the milkman's wife had received weekly bulletins from her husband who was stationed at Langemarck and had written every day; and Albert's wife was fighting in Sergeant Edgington's RHA Battery at Neuve Chapelle and wrote long letters about the severe casualties they were suffering.

Marigold, who had decided she had to get away for a while, was off to Wales and the following day Alice accompanied her to Paddington station. The engine drew away and a cloud of steam engulfed the platform, masking the unexpected tears that flowed down to her earlobes in rivers. Another bond to Edward had been severed. This fragile, fussy lady, with her odd walk and high laugh had been at variance with her on so many occasions, but now that she was gone Alice felt the diminishing of her existence even more deeply.

That night she settled at her writing desk. As the nib scraped upon the paper, every phrase, every word was accompanied by an almost imperceptible flicker in her face, as a change of tempo in an emotional symphony.

'Dear Sirs, I beg to acknowledge the receipt of your communication and in reply I am at a loss what to believe. What am I to tell his mother? I write to request a meeting with your commanding officer at the earliest opportunity. Yours sincerely, Alice Sanderson.'

With a trembling hand she signed the letter. A determined control of her feelings had hardened into a willful denial.

When she slumped back in her chair the room was dark save for the small glow cast by the gas lamp. She folded the letter into the envelope and then sat looking out of the window, watching the shadows careering across the moon and listening to the soughing of the wind.

Within the week, with the assistance of Edward's father who pulled some vital strings, an invitation came to visit the Barracks in person. She arrived mid-morning, and Oscar Garwood, the Commander of Edward's Regiment, received her immediately into his office.

Garwood, a short, barrel-bodied gentleman, gazed at Alice and appeared not to have registered what she told him.

Around them the building swarmed with activity. A new generation of Kitchener's Army was being trained, and through an open window came the sounds of the morning drill.

After several minutes, the officer who was standing outside entered, ushering in a thin, puny-looking man who shuffled awkwardly, dazzled by the glare of his seniors. When he heard the Commander wanted to speak to him, his anxious eyes reverted to panic. Perhaps he thought they were going to discipline him.

'Do you know my husband, Edward Sanderson?' asked Alice, her voice wavering.

'Yes, Madam,' said the Private, his face white. He shot a nervous glance at the Commander.

The other officer said nothing.

'I was near Essex Farm and around there, about two miles from HQ, you know, the house…'

'Around there' meant the area surrounding Sanctuary Wood where the Second Oxford and Bucks were fighting.

'HQ? You mean the White Chateau?' Garwood, sitting down, corrected him with a questioning raised eyebrow.

Again the young Private looked edgeways at his superior officer, who evidently had a reputation for order among the trainee soldiers.

Garwood thoughtfully placed the ash from his cigar into the small silver ashtray sitting on his desk.

'You were fighting alongside my husband?' said Alice, egging him on.

'Yes, madam…' He took a step backwards, as if ashamed of his boots, which were not polished. He continued. 'I remember it clearly. As soon as it was light the Germans opened with all guns. Lots of men were halted in their tracks, but we got out. At about 3 p.m., I saw their company retreating. This was the absolute devil, as I had to get out and rush along to report. They told me to retire and stop the Germans getting past the road. From then, as soon as we left the field they opened on us with every gun and rifle. We got back, and neither of my officers was hit. I assumed the new position and collected about a hundred and fifty men. Things were getting tricky, as the Germans by this time were pouring through the gap in the hedge and filling up the wood…'

He shifted uneasily. Suddenly finding his confidence, he stared at Alice as if in a trance, apparently struck by her beauty. He seemed not to understand the effect the story was having on her.

He went on.

'Under the circumstances I decided that to do

something unexpected might upset their applecart, so we fixed bayonets and went straight in.'

'And 7th Company?'

He looked at the ceiling, as if trying not to draw attention to his boots. 'No sign of 'em, sir. We assumed they'd bought it. It was dark when we got back to the barracks. By then we'd annihilated about fifty of the grey swine. Only twenty-three of my company left, sir.'

'And my husband. Did he return with you?'

The two soldiers remained silent.

'Then, do you think him dead?'

After a pause that felt extremely long the Commander said, 'I have already spoken with the General. If there is anything more, we will know in a few days.' He stubbed out his cigar.

Alice extended her hand.

'Thank you and goodbye, sir.'

He nodded and smiled, and the Private turned on his heel to go back to the drill.

'Thank you,' said Alice, but he didn't look back.

'It's a filthy war,' said the Commander as they parted.

Alice nodded.

Chapter 6

The prisoner's camp was damp and crowded and there were no washing facilities. In the unheated sleeping huts men slept on makeshift bunks under filthy blankets and the British and French rubbed shoulders with German criminals. Work was in the fields or in the timber yards where beds and tables were constructed, but the real demand was for coffins. The war in Flanders had caused a rush.

The prisoners' diet consisted of bread, although the guards enjoyed cabbages, boiled to oblivion, pickled in vinegar and tasting of brine. Cigarettes and sausages were bought in the town, although even tobacco was subject to rationing. Despite the official prohibition of alcohol, Schiffer, a tall, lean fox-faced youth, obtained brandy on the sly. The guards still considered themselves hard done by.

Edward did not join in with the men who whistled to keep going. He felt ashamed at his capture. His once clean-shaven chin was bearded, his hair long about his ears. His face bore the sorrow that buried itself there, deep in the folds of the tiny, fresh wrinkles.

He picked up his plank and made his way to the workshop, weaving among the hammering and chiselling, his hands stinging as if he were holding burning iron. The saw and plane had blistered his palms and painful callouses were forming. They were a musician's hands no more.

Watson had aged even more noticeably. His baby smile

had faded and a soulful, dark emptiness filled his eyes. Only Fitzroy seemed his usual withdrawn self.

Stone, whose chest condition had deteriorated, was coughing blood, but Major Stern, the commandant, ignored him. Stern walked with a limp, a wound he reported dated from the Franco-Prussian war. He seemed an intelligent man, with his wry smile and watchful beady eyes, and blind to the harsh conditions over which he had little control.

As a token of his respect and goodwill, he allowed the prisoners to visit the town once or twice every week, provided they were accompanied. Officially the outings were to collect supplies, but often the young guards led their prisoners to a tavern. The captives attended to their sacks of grain and flour, while the guards filled their beer glasses and admired the local women.

Edward, seeing these girls in their bright dresses, felt nothing more than curiosity. He saw in them only imperfection, while Alice remained on the lofty pedestal of his thoughts. On the few occasions he found himself alone he would close his eyes and images of her flooded into his memory. He pictured her beautiful mouth, the soft contours of her breast, the curves of her calves. He heard her playing her harp, watched her smooth knuckles whitening as her fragile hands brushed across the strings. Then he remembered that anonymous letter.

He cast the memory aside, and felt safe again. In the dim recesses of his mind he would remember his father's reproaches and hear his mother's nagging, and then he would see their doting looks.

If only he had written more than the few inadequate postcards he had sent before his capture. Prisoners were supposed to be able to send and receive mail, although any correspondence was censored, and in reality, the guards could not be bothered to forward the letters that would no doubt incriminate them and pass on secrets and lies directly to their enemy.

The icy temperatures affected the spirits of the group and made them feel dejected. It rained incessantly and the roof leaked. A few transitory bright spells followed, but then a low fog enveloped the countryside. Soon white frost covered the land.

Breakfast was the usual thick, gloopy porridge. Peter Stone had disappeared and no one knew where he had gone. Perhaps Peak, his orderly, was looking after the sick man. Perhaps he was dead. Nothing surprised Edward any more.

Fitzroy sat opposite Edward. His shrewd, alert eyes sparkled, for he knew Edward was plotting something. He stroked his bony chin, on which a coat of rough stubble was lengthening, and his eyes followed Edward's attentively.

Edward smiled. For the first time in weeks he found himself able to hope. The irony was that none other than Fitzroy had inspired him.

After a long, studied pause Edward began to speak. 'I have to get out of here…' He glanced around, drew his chair closer and lowered his voice. 'There must be a way.' He clenched his fist and banged it on the table. During his three months of imprisonment an intense store of repressed determination had built up within him and it was about to explode.

Not one man had managed to escape so far. The perimeters were guarded and at night dogs barked in the darkness around the fence.

Fitzroy frowned. 'Edward, their spies are everywhere.'

Edward did not respond. Their eyes remained fixed on

each other. Then Fitzroy made a gesture as if to say, 'Well, I'm right, am I not?'

Edward shook his head. He had an idea. He had seen the band of musicians as they tuned their instruments before playing in front of the crowds of locals. These drummers, accordion-players and singers were a background accompaniment to drinking. 'I am willing to take a chance.'

He felt delirious with a sense of purpose. Knife in hand, he could willingly carve a path across the bodies of men if he had to. In a low voice, he articulated his plan.

'When?' said Fitzroy.

'Wednesday ...' Edward had to think before he answered. He had lost track of time. None knew how long it had been since their capture, because the guards would not tell them. The cold that told him it was not summer, but he had no idea which month.

Fitzroy could see in Edward's face not only the disorientation, but the cool, courageous calm and steady resolve that Edward himself was surprised to have felt in himself. Maturity told the older man not to try talking the younger out of it. Desperation told each he had to offer his trust without reservation.

When the two men left the table Watson was at the doorway. The brief looks that they exchanged were enough to make Edward realize that he and Fitzroy had been overheard. For two of them to escape successfully would require guile. Watson, who understood that a decoy was needed, was determined to help without any consideration for his own safety.

The three of them argued in whispers, as the tips of their cigarettes shone like miniscule stars in the brown winter gloom.

If

The following day the prisoners set off on their march into town as usual, accompanied by their armed captors. Lieutenant Hirsch prodded them along with his pistol, his lopsided, immobile face brightening as they approached the Auberge de Meuse. Faint strains of a Flemish folk melody were transported on the still, crisp air. Edward did not recognize the tune, but he was ready to play.

Chapter 7

It was a savage irony that while humanity was torn apart, nature seemed oblivious to the carnage. Primroses and crocuses studded the grasses of the gardens in Cheyne Walk. White fluff bent the boughs of the apple trees, and the magnolias had turned pale pink.

The intense, agonizing fire of longing with which Alice had previously counted the days to Edward's homecoming had burned away, leaving a dull, lingering ache. With no concrete news of his whereabouts, she clung on without expectation, lest a new disappointment should cast her into a fresh whirlpool of despair. At the same time, she was unable to grieve.

For brief intervals she became aware of the joy in the rain-washed sky and plump clouds. She accepted the invitation to dinner with the Countess after all.

Seated opposite her, Helga Coberg surveyed her guests gracefully. Alice recognized the Countess immediately. Her face was kind, and behind the translucent skin a network of violet hairline veins were visible. Her slender, delicate frame was like a rose that had bloomed and fallen. She had been at the party where Alice had met Edward.

Around them, seated at the great dining table, about twenty guests chatted among themselves. The men were dressed in black tie or uniform, the women in evening gowns decorated with jewels. No one might have guessed the country was at war.

To Alice's right sat a middle-aged gentleman who had drooping jowls that wobbled slightly as he pontificated about the Germans in a clipped voice. Sitting to her left was an elegant lady in peacock-blue silk and diamond earrings. They exchanged a few irrelevant sentences and Alice answered her questions about the hospital as honestly as possible, aware her comments served only as a pretext to give the lady the opportunity of examining her.

'Do you think the war will be over soon?' asked Alice.

The lady, not wishing to engage too earnestly on the unavoidable subject that both unsettled and terrified her, tidied the food on her plate to one side with her fork.

Alice, glancing around the table, could find no other face she recognized, though one or two seemed familiar. Throughout the first and second courses she noticed one of the guests, who sat at the other side of the table some distance away, glanced often in her direction. Their eyes met several times. He was a strongly built man with a fine moustache and wearing an officer's uniform. His shiny full cheeks reflected a healthy appetite for life, rendering the sadness in his eyes more poignant.

The man who had been transfixed by her during dinner was now suddenly beside her.

'Forgive me,' said the stranger. 'May I speak with you?'

His tone was so urgent that Alice immediately felt anxious. 'Of course,' she said.

'My name is Charles Spicer...' he said and in a slow, quiet, measured voice he relayed the story of Evangeline's death without pausing once for breath.

Alice's composure failed her. She put the glass down, hid the whiteness of her face in her hands and whispered, 'When?'

'Last month.'

'You were there?'

'No, but I heard the account from my Second Officer.'

'How did she die?' She gazed at him almost accusingly, this man who had taken her poor, defenseless, unmarried friend and put her in danger.

'Evangeline was very brave. She was carrying a message for Whitehall .'

Alice riveted her eyes on his and he paused. Deep furrows carved into his brow and she could not unravel his expression, which seemed conflicted and confused.

'What message was that?'

He shook his head. 'She loved you dearly. She thought she had upset you.' Spicer spoke the words with confidence. 'And you? What is your story?'

'I fear it is not yet written,' said Alice.

Chapter 8

Autumn had relieved the trees of their brown, dried burdens, and a bitter Siberian wind swept across the countryside. The fields flooded with rain had become quagmires, but the prisoners, whatever their former rank or nationality, were still commanded to dig up the potato harvest. Here and there, patches of white ice were still visible, floating at the frozen edges of the fields. Snow began to swirl in wild, huge flakes.

The men worked silently, and their breath rose in clouds of steam as they began pushing with their shovels. The jackets they had been given were too thin and their boots leaked.

Weak and exhausted, Edward pushed back his hair as it fell on to his forehead. He fell to his knees and wrenched the potato root out, lifting it up as if it were trophy. This was the day he had been waiting for. Freedom was so near that he could smell it.

He could see only three guards. Schiffer, in his thick wool overcoat, watched the men dig. He leant on his rifle, from time to time barking instructions at them. Two other guards stood idly chatting and smoking. Stern was nowhere to be seen. Edward assumed he would be along later.

Late afternoon the sacks were loaded and the horses, harnessed to carts from which bells dangled hauled their cargo willingly. Some of the crop was to be sold to shopkeepers, some was to be traded at market.

Only the guards rode. The prisoners were made to go on foot. The dense tide of the crowd surged around them and only a muffled, confused murmur issued from its midst. The faces were benign rather than antagonistic, as the prisoners had first assumed.

Between the German bayonets the kind hands of French women offered food parcels to the passing men.

'*Prenez...pour vous...*' The elderly lady called out, her tear-stained eyes shining in her withered face.

Edward took the cotton bag and something stirred in him. She was a stranger, yet he recognized clearly in her pleading, compassionate expression the heart of his own mother.

They paused at the tavern to allow the guards to take their break. Stern arrived to oversee the unloading. The prisoners were to remain outside in the yard.

Edward peeked inside the door, into the primitive smoke-filled room that stank of beer. A band was playing a popular folk song, but the lively, happy playing only intensified the illusion.

Fitzroy's quick nod told him that neither would deviate from the plan. Fitzroy continued with the distraction they had agreed, and, as Watson dropped to the ground, pretending to have injured his leg, the guards ran to him and Edward silently slipped away.

From the front doorway his eyes frantically scanned the musty back room filled with crates and boxes and scattered with instrument cases. A double bass stood propped up against a barrel and a tambourine. At that moment he spotted the fiddle, lying on a table in the far corner. His heart began to race.

Keeping low, he slid deftly behind the pile of coats. Then, his knees trembling, he moved to the table and picked up the bow, smoothing with his forefinger the silky, fine horsehair. Almost inaudibly, he plucked the strings to check if it was tuned. The peg squeaked painfully as he adjusted it.

Beads of sweat broke out on the back of his neck. It was now or never. He stood up straight, strode into the bar and took up his position at the back behind the other musicians, half-expecting to be recognized as an intruder. To his astonishment, no one seemed to register the stranger in their midst – or the violin. The bassoonist even gave him a welcoming nod.

The adrenalin kicked in straight away. For the first few bars Edward mimed. Then, willing his fingers not to shake, he mustered all his courage and began. He reached for the G sharp and under-reached the note. He glanced around in panic. To his relief, no one appeared to have noticed. In the middle of his confused, frenzied thoughts he saw another audience clapping and cheering. The throng of smiling faces felt encouraging, benevolent even. By some miracle, his fumbling fingers seemed to steady. He played on, out of amazement as much as fear, his instinct to cry out and, as the chorus came around a second time, his chest began to swell.

Suddenly, he was somewhere else. He imagined himself on another stage and at another time – in England. In his mind he saw the Professor and his mother. The thousands of hours of striving and practice all seemed worthwhile. So this was it, he thought to himself. A lump rose to his throat at the realization that he needed no gun or any other weapon to free himself. Music was the key to his own victory. It always had been.

He had no idea how long he had been playing when, out of the corner of his eye he glimpsed Stern and Schiffer, tankards in hands, rosy-cheeked, eyes glistening, as they slurred words he did not understand.

When Watson had distracted the guards and Edward had slunk inside the tavern, Fitzroy had left the yard and, without anyone noticing, even Watson, he had crept slyly into the barn. There he remained hidden, crouched beneath a haystack, shivering violently, waiting for Edward. Face hidden in his folded arms, he spoke voiceless yet impassioned prayers with the congregation of horses, sheep and oxen. Rowdy shouts and the occasional clanking of beer glasses could be heard amid the faint strains of reedy stringed instruments. Outside in the yard, there was hardly a noise coming from the exhausted prisoners. He wondered if one or two had fallen asleep.

The clock struck ten. Fitzroy's palms began to sweat and his head throbbed. He was debating with himself whether to move nearer the exit when the guards, having consumed enough beer to sink the British naval fleet, could be heard drunkenly rounding the prisoners up and issuing instructions.

He buried himself in straw, his chest pounding. He heard footsteps. Someone had entered the barn. He peeked his head around and one of the horses neighed. Voices echoed in the distance. A rat scuttled on the cobbles. Then there was nothing, only the steady clip-clop of horses' hooves as the ponies were led off. Was someone still in there? It was too dark to tell. His hand reached for the pitchfork and he knelt, motionless, ready to pounce.

Inside the tavern the rowdy singing had died down and the musicians took their bow. For a split second, Edward stood basking in the glory, before he wiped the silly smile from his face. He glanced nervously across the clapping hands and saw Stern and the others making their exit.

Violin still in hand, he ducked behind the accordion player and retreated quickly into the back room behind a pile of beer barrels. Only when he was certain that the coast was clear did he make a run for it.

Once out in the yard, Edward turned, listening, but heard nothing. Then, as he followed the shadows into the barn to Fitzroy, he imagined he heard barking dogs, but there was no sign of any guards and his fellow prisoners.

Inside the barn he was met with the pitchfork. 'Calm down!' Fitzroy put the weapon down, torn between anger and relief. Hunched together, side by side, the two men hid for several hours, too afraid to whisper. Distant voices grew loud and then faded and suddenly a torch beam darted near the doorway. Edward's leg moved involuntarily. Fitzroy put his finger on his mouth and both men they were done for. The torchlight swept the barn again, resting on the oxen. This time it was Edward who said a prayer. As the beam darted away in the other direction, he could not help but give thanks.

By midnight a fine mist hung in the air. Everything around them was in darkness and the silence floated empty and lifeless. Stretching their cramped, stiff limbs, they crawled through the outer door of the barn, their sombre coarse clothes blending with the night. Breathlessly, they scrambled to the fence and began to sprint, but the ground was sodden and uneven and Edward stumbled. Twice his leg became trapped in the mud. He was not as strong as Fitzroy, or as nimble, but even the athletic Fitzroy fell over.

Somehow they reached the edge of the field where they followed the willows upstream. They turned for one last look at the camp, and as the smudged outline of its shabby rafters began to emerge in the blue light, forced themselves on.

'Amiens?' Fitzroy's mouth spun steam into the wet air.

The pale moon, hard and empty, seemed to lead the way as it hung suspended before them. They hastened on, their trousers jangling with coins, their pockets bulging with apples, and from somewhere in the vast, unknown distance the wind blew towards them the charred, poisonous air of the battlefields.

They did not dare remain around Sedan, lest anyone recognize them, but the situation was more complicated, for they understood there were spies working for Germany almost everywhere and it was safer to go on foot.

The weather, however, was against them. Sometimes the country tracks vanished beneath their boots and the entire landscape grew so waterlogged that it became a marshland. They were frequently caught in torrential downpours that seemed as if they would drown them, the water beating them, drawing at them, pulling them down into the sodden earth.

Occasionally small hamlets or farmsteads would rise like beacons. Whenever they could they jumped on the back of carts, when they were thrown about topsy-turvy with pigs, sheep, goats and cattle.

In the village of Brogny, in the vicinity of Ardennes, catkins hung low from the bare, black branches, and in the damp woods between Braux and Levrezy swallows sang. The stable appeared empty, its door ajar. The farmer, Pierre, saw no need to lock it. He was a simple man who lived quietly with his wife and two horses. Every evening he settled himself for hours by the river, watching the grebes and little bitterns.

It was a blessing that Pierre Meriel had offered them shelter. The two men cut wood, carried water and fed chickens. In return they had received warm clothes, new boots and twenty-five francs.

A small fissure hardly larger than a fist and covered by a thin piece of jagged glass let in the pink light. Among the shadows the occasional nicker or snort could be heard from the horses.

From the back of the mound of hay came the low hum of voices.

'So what about your daughter?'

'She stayed at the house and became a teacher,' said Fitzroy to Edward.

'And she speaks French too?'

Fitzroy nodded. 'She is clever – and pretty, although her eyebrows are a little bushy – like mine!' As if to prove the point he frowned, kitting them effortlessly into one thick, hairy line.

After a few moments Edward said, 'My wife has beautiful eyebrows. She plays the harp.'

That morning the sun tried to peek through the clouds. In fear for their lives, they hiked across the bleak countryside, along deserted tracks and through copses, with hope in their hearts. Whenever they passed a stranger they nodded, smiled casually and carried on. Underneath, like all actors, they remained seized by terror.

As night fell the two men continued to muse in the gloom, while around them with air was strong with the smell of manure. At least the icy chill could not reach them here and, for a few days at least, they could exchange anecdotes about life back home, with all the promise that it held for them.

They had hoped to take the train to Amiens and from there cross to Calais without delay.

It was when hiding in the back of one of these jolty, rickety farm vehicles that they had come across Pierre

Meriel. Meriel hated the war and the Germans with an even greater passion. He was a pacifist.

Meriel offered them shelter immediately. He knew that they were British war prisoners. Marie, his wife, a muscly, full-bosomed woman, offered them onion soup and bacon. 'You can sleep in the house,' she told them.

In reality they preferred the stable. It was warm and there was less snoring than if they were to share a room with two octogenarians.

But they could not stay long. The two men said their farewells and carried on, this time armed with a pistol. They walked for a while and soon caught a ride with grain sacks. The driver of the cart remained oblivious. Edward looked down at the mud lashing against the rusted cart's wheels as they jangled and pictured Alice's hair loose and falling about her shoulders. He could feel her locket dancing in his breast pocket. He recalled the tiniest details of their life together, the way she arranged her slippers and left his where they were lying, how she loved to wind up his watch for him. A tumult of conflicting thoughts surged through his mind, from the second he had first set eyes on her to the one where they had parted. How long had it been since that day? He had no idea.

In his exhausted heart he clung to the memory of the woman he loved, with her russet-gold hair and long white fingers, her head bent forward in concentration, a barely perceptible blush tinting her otherwise pale cheeks. 'Alice…' he said out loud, as something inside him began to crack. No matter how fast he traveled through the driving, stabbing rain there was no escape from the sweet turmoil of his love for her. It emerged as light from the cloying, sucky, molten ground. It was a butterfly scent that fluttered along the summer land that he had forsaken. It flowed in wild, scorching flames.

That night, as the two men huddled in the barn of Henri Lapin, a blacksmith who lived at Peronne, Edward made use of the pen and paper Marie Meriel had given him and began a letter to his wife.

'I'm sorry I didn't write. I didn't know how. I was confused. It was as if those months when you were mine were not real. Do you still love me? Do you remember me? This is the one thought that gives me strength – that you still wait for me. If I should ever learn that you have forgotten me and given yourself to another, it would break me.'

Heart brimming, he folded the paper and put it in his pocket with the necklace. He rested his head on a straw bale, overwhelmed by the turbulence that possessed him.

His plan was straightforward, albeit naïve and ambitious. They would board the train after it had left the station that evening. Carriages crammed with the enemy rolled through the bitter desolation that ran from east to west, away from the front entirely, but the trains were empty in the evenings and it was easier to move in the dark.

Dressed as farmworkers, at first the two privates did nothing to arouse suspicion as they arrived in Amiens. Heads lowered, they made their way through Gothic streets lined with troubadour houses. They crossed over a canal, and Edward scoured the streets for a postbox, but his frantic searching was in vain and the letter to Alice remained in his breast pocket, warmed by his fiercely beating heart.

In the cobbled street they bought croissants. Armed German soldiers were everywhere – huddling in groups, buying cigarettes, and chatting to locals. They slipped casually into a small garden where they proposed to await the departure of the night train. Only then did they notice the exquisite window, its stoned glass harnessing the light, which cascaded in honeyed shafts on to the plants and bushes. They had stumbled on the cathedral entirely by accident. With its vast flying buttresses and piercing spire, the great church felt like a heaven-sent sanctuary, and it was the perfect place to hide.

As they hurried up the steps and into the nave, Edward could not say why exactly his glance strayed to the girl who, with her simple clothes and beret pulled down tightly around her ears attracted his attention. He couldn't even see her properly. He looked at her and she glanced across casually as one might steal a look at any stranger.

Fitzroy tugged his sleeve.

For the remainder of the afternoon they sat on one of the wooden benches at the back of the side chapel, pulled the peaks of their caps over their faces and prepared to wait it out.

Fitzroy's head dropped occasionally onto his shoulder and he began to doze. Soon Edward fell asleep too. What was that?

A heavy hand fell on Fitzroy's back and a tall Commandant, his face scarred with pockmarks, stood glaring at them.

'*Ihre Dokumenten, bitte!*'

Edward felt his courage evaporate.

Fitzroy looked the man straight in the eye and in schoolboy French said, '*Ils sont a la maison...*'

The Commandant showed no emotion at this unlikely explanation. With a slight jerk of the head he indicated the door.

'Go! You are coming with me!'

Edward launched into a sentence that made little sense.

Fitzroy, looming over the German soldier, persisted with his attempts. 'What do you want of us? We are workers.' He raised and opened his hands and showed his empty palms. 'Look – we have no weapons – let us go.'

The Hun leaned forward and snarled, '*Englander*?'

Edward looked away.

The German measured them with his glance. 'You are going home to attack us again?' he said in English.

Edward wanted to respond, but the man had a pistol and he was directing it at his face.

'*S'il vous plait…*' Fitzroy's tone became instantly conciliatory. He was eyeing the barrel.

But the German was having none of it. They started walking and the Hun followed them four paces to the rear, indicating the direction they were to march. The military headquarters was located at the post office, commandeered in the occupation.

As they walked another German soldier joined them. The two Germans exchanged a few words.

Fitzroy took the opportunity to whisper to Edward, 'As soon as we reach that corner....'

'Over there?' Edward whispered.

'No, there…' Fitzroy nodded in the other direction, towards the copse.

Scarcely had they gone twenty yards when Fitzroy stopped dead in his tracks. He turned around and without hesitation struck the man on the chin with his bare fist. At the impact of his punch the officer's groan echoed. He staggered and then fell. Edward took the pistol tucked into his boot and fired. He had no idea if the shot had missed.

They ran from the street towards the wood, as fast as their legs would carry them. As they went, cries broke out in the distance and a succession of shots popped.

Underfoot, the mossy softness gave way to prickly, damp thorns. He could sense Fitzroy stumbling alongside him. He could hear water.

Undeterred, he thundered on, until he felt his chest would burst. He stopped, struggling to catch his breath, and his jelly legs gave way beneath him. As he fell to his knees, from somewhere nearby, he heard a low thud. He turned around but, despite the hazy glow of the crescent moon, could see nothing clearly between the latticework of eerie black branches. He listened carefully, but no sound penetrated the silence except the thumping, deafening blows of his too-loud heart.

It was a long, long time before his breathing steadied and he saw the shadows grow into a hunched mass lying on the ground. It was like a branch, this motionless heap, with the arm twisted back, the eyes staring, the small crucifix glinting about the neck.

It was Fitzroy and he was dead.

PART III
1916–1917

Chapter 1

Perched on the windowsill, Alice watched, transfixed as down below, two men in overalls carried the Coberg's grand piano out of the building on straps. The keyboard and lid were sealed down with tape, the feet were covered in a blue velvet cloth and they had padded the guide strings. Ivy, the maid, was nowhere to be seen.

Alice had not felt that she had many things in common with the Professor and his wife, but her heart shuddered with a surprising force at the realization that they were leaving. It was as if the furniture of her past was going with them. The carefree, innocent girl she had once been had gone, along with it all delusions.

Of course, it was for the best. No one with any connection to Germany or Austria could feel safe. The Austrian bakery, the only place that still sold reasonably fresh bread, had had its windows smashed in.

'Your end first! Watch out!' One of the men put down the instrument. Wisps of grey hair protruded from his cloth cap. She could hear every word. The other man, hooked-nosed and snowy-bearded, gazed up with lowering and contracted brows, but failed to notice her and the offending pigeon, having alighted on a sill on the third floor, appeared to be minding its own business.

The man wearing the cap had disappeared suddenly. Leaning on the piano as if it might prop him up, his mate began to whistle.

Alice wiped the tear away with her taut, damp hand.

Watching the piano filled her with unimaginable sorrow. She had not touched the harp since they had clinked glasses to 1916. It seemed to her now like an exquisite relic, a memorial to lost innocence.

Down below, the other removal man had returned. He was still catching his breath. He wiped his brow with his sleeve. Clearly he was struggling. Much to Alice's relief, the other one had finished his slightly flat rendition of 'Dinky Parlay Voo'.

She listened to the sickly, ironic, piercing melody she knew off pat. However cheerful it sounded, it was impossible to pretend everything was well in the world. Sir Charles Spicer had been killed at Verdun.

Her thoughts returned inevitably to her husband. Perhaps, by some inconceivable stroke of fate, he could be alive. What would it be like if, out of nowhere, he suddenly reappeared? How would they ever rescue their shattered, paralyzed married life after so long?

With the greatest of difficulty, the two men had dragged the instrument up the ramp, heaving and pushing. Now they were leaving.

Leaning her head against the glass pane, Alice watched them go, safe behind these walls that shielded her from this awful world and the people that it had snatched from her. Her only respite had been the coming spring and warmer weather; and last week she had dined at Rules with her old friend Jasper.

She was grateful for the overcrowded ward at the hospital and its patients because they deprived her of the opportunity for selfishness. There were at the last count fifty-two beds of acute surgical cases in a state of crisis and they certainly put matters into perspective.

Sister was a large-boned, crimson-faced lady dressed in a suitable uniform of black trimmed with white cuffs and collar, with darned black stockings and sensible lace-ups. Her features were not given to smiling, but her face had bestowed an inward pleasantry as she cordially, due to the acute short staffing at the hospital, suggested that Alice was to assist in one of newly equipped makeshift operating theatres.

The atmosphere was chaotic and desperate, but Alice was ready for the debilitating schedule and thankless toil, even though her patriotism had worn thin. The consequences of Loos could be plainly seen, delivered in hospital ships and trains bulging to bursting point, but the consequences of Ypres, where Edward had been stationed, were less obvious. In the recesses of her mind, a small part of her half-expected her dear, lost, beautiful Edward to be brought in one day.

Abject terror dominated her first day in the operating theatre. The procedure began in a converted basement chamber that had formerly been a storeroom. Her scrubbed hands in their new rubber gloves were at the ready beside the tray of boiled surgical instruments, her body turned a little to the side, and she stood without exactly looking into the incision and the small area of naked shining red.

The surgeon appeared to recognize her emotion. He stood calmly opposite her, his hand thrust deep into the chest of the patients. He was tall, slender and unusual-looking. He had an intriguing face, its smooth brow glowed a little on an almost equine-shaped head.

After it was over and the operating team had left the scrub room, he introduced himself. 'I have been hoping to meet you for some time,' he said.

She looked at him in surprise. 'Do we know each

other?' she asked, unable to disguise her relief that the patient, who was badly wounded, had survived.

Although it was impossible to tell from first impressions, Dr Sebastian Peterson struck her as an intelligent man. He had an open, honest face. His eyes pierced her with their enigmatic curiosity.

'We met once,' he said.

'Are you sure? Where?'.

'At a concert. I was at school with Harry Lloyd.' He enveloped Alice in a surreptitious glance, from her flat lace-up shoes to her hair that shone like a rust-copper lily.

'Really?' Alice frowned. She couldn't recall him.

'Yes,' said the doctor, 'but it was a long time ago.'

As they strolled along the corridor, a light flush filled Alice's cheeks and neck, which, together with her smile, only animated her beauty.

'Have you heard from Harry?'

'He is in Thiepval.' Peterson pulled out a cigarette case, snapped open the lid of the exquisite silver box, and offered it to Alice.

'I don't smoke,' she said, as if assembling her memories.

'And did you ever meet my husband, Harry's friend?'

'I heard him play the violin. And I heard you once.'

He looked at her with a different eye, an eye that wished to delve deep inside her learn the secret power that was rocking her. Its inner calm seemed to rise from the depths of his being, and its scrutiny seemed as if it might be able to touch the very wounds that the hands had been engaged in repairing. A kindness was reflected in the depth of that expression, as well as sadness.

Alice, somewhat shyly, leaned away. She glanced at his hands. There was, she thought, more elegance and distinction in them than she had seen in any musician's. As lonely and bereft as she felt, she could not bring herself to say anything about Edward. It felt almost a betrayal to do so and inappropriate. Politely, she excused herself, thinking it best to seek refuge in silence.

After her shift she walked home alone, wondering about Edward. Had distance and war severed the ties between her and the young man who had filled her heart and imagination? If she tried hard enough she could still picture his face, although pieces were missing from the jigsaw of his smile.

Then she saw Sebastian Peterson as he had appeared to her in the hospital operating theatre. Impressions of him gnawed at her – his odd, handsome face, his wild hair extended behind his ears in feathery flaps and his low, grainy voice, his pale, interesting eyes.

Here was a new question, no matter how hard she tried to dismiss it, and a new shock even though it had already penetrated her very bones, but the only answer she received was a warning. Her searing longing for peace and security kept getting buffeted by the despair of not knowing and the hopes fluttering in the air.

How did love fit in with all this? Something had shifted inside her, although would not admit it to herself. With feigned indifference, she hummed cheerfully as she made her way past Arch House Wharf, just as a nightingale's drowsy, syncopated notes heralded the night.

Chapter 2

Panting like a dog, tears spidery on his cold cheeks, Edward had no choice but to run through the broken twigs that wanted to pin him back. He ran until the dim light wrung the last blue-grey tinge out of the stars, dripping darkly between the trees. Only now was he ashamed, He was pierced through with it. He tried to cry but his throat ached without a whisper. The other sounds he could not prevent: the rook's alarm call and the pop of the motorbike as he kick-started the pedal with his foot.

He shook the bike from side to side to see if it contained petrol. A light swish of liquid emanated from the tank. He slammed it into first, legs dangling at either side, and as he released his grip and accelerated along the muddy track and down towards the deserted white road, he felt a giddy whirl of confused freedom. An ordinary stranger in an unknown territory, he did not know France or Belgium, or where he was going.

He had dragged Fitzroy's body into full view so it would be found. In a sweaty panic, at first he had considered burying it, but this way seemed better, and one that might offer the man the chance of a decent burial. These thoughts were all fleeting, for in the heat of the moment his mind seemed hardly to function at all.

The further he drove, the more isolated and exposed he felt. On the low rise of inclines once or twice he could make out the grey triangles of churches, thin sentinel trees and the odd cluster of a smallholding, but for the most part he saw only the same flat, unchanging landscape, apparently uninhabited, whose acrid brown soil had been undergoing the same ancient ritual of growth and decay as it had done for millennia.

But the enemy was behind the line and the only soldiers in this region were allies. The engine whined and spluttered, and as the green fields passed, it was as if he was still in England, with its fresh, crisp, green agricultural patchwork, so peaceful and timeless did the countryside appear. He wanted to stop and sleep, right there at the roadside. Instead, he held on tight to the handlebars, breathed the cold air deeply and concentrated.

In his imagination he was playing the violin. It was something by Elgar, a sonata perhaps, although he could not recall the exact piece. Alice was watching him and she was smiling. He saw the feathery hairs on her forearm as they prickled and the small, almost indiscernible mole on her left shoulder, just above the arm, where no one else could see it, not even she herself.

At the village station he propped the bike against the wall, walked briskly to the ticket office and bought a ticket. He saw how the station officer's eyes ran him up and down him. He saw, beneath the cheery good manners, how they registered his foreignness. What was that strange, unmistakable Britishness that emanated from him and gave him away? Or was it the stench of rats and blood that seemed to trigger suspicion? Perhaps he looked unkempt? He put his hand to his chin, but there was only a small residue of bristle that had grown back after he had shaved at the Lapin's.

Automatically he put his hand to the knife tucked into his inner jacket, recalling the typed message from

Kitchener once folded in his pay book reminding him to be courteous, considerate and kind to the local people. He attempted a little French, and the French ticket officer smiled him a wry smile and wished him a pleasant journey.

When the train arrived, the thin haunted creatures who sat in the carriages were not the men with shiny polished boots and hopeful faces that had set off from Victoria Station. These expressions were vacant, but they were still British, proud and resilient, and the uniforms were worn and mud-spattered.

It was strange to have time to notice corn like powdered gold over the fields. The sun was jagged through the window and so luminous the spangles turned red and flowed, dried-blood in his eyes.

Upon arrival at Rouen he worked his way through the crowds, heady with hope and exhaustion. A ship was steaming up to the wharf and a military band was playing. Children with emaciated white faces and wearing black aprons clung to the skirts of their mothers. Pausing on the cobbled crossroads, he watched British soldiers and nurses and the thousand waving Union Jacks. With drums and fifes blaring, the throng cried out, '*Vive les Anglais!*'

It was his last franc, but he was only too happy to buy the postcard from the kiosk. He wanted to remember this moment forever.

It must have been about seven in the evening, but the sky was still light and the globe of the sun hung low above the jumble of narrow medieval streets and higgledy-piggledy dwellings. With not a centime in his pocket, a dusty grey ambulance carried him to a grand house decorated with glittering chandeliers. The mansion was the new battalion HQ. One could not help admiring the commander's taste.

He woke with a start and looked at the wall clock with bewilderment. He had slept for seven hours and was still wearing the same clothes, ragged and torn and caked with sweat and Fitzroy's blood. Sunlight streamed into the stark, empty room.

If he tried hard he could draw with his gaze the dusky outline of a woman's face, but it was not her whole face, just her pale, imploring, beseeching eyes. Did it belong to Alice? He couldn't say exactly. Everything else was a blur – her voice, her gestures, how she moved.

All he could see was Fitzroy, lying there immobile, with his thick, heavy bones and fixed staring gaze. It felt unbearable that he had not been able to bury his friend properly.

He washed and shaved and after a fresh change of clothes, felt less weak. He sat staring into space, not knowing where to begin or how to explain himself, as ill-prepared as any prisoner for an inquisition.

The wind's chill made it impossible to sit outside. In the community room a small group of officers in residence gathered on the sofas and armchairs.

Major Tennyson motioned them to be quiet.

'Please begin with the day you were taken.'

Edward glanced around at the circle of expectant faces. In a hoarse voice, he began with the day at Lys. Clearing his throat, he moved on to the camp, naming who else had been captured. Greeted with understanding nods, he acquired a little more confidence. He talked about the tuberculosis and the cholera and the havoc among the soldiers, the mouldy oatmeal and the pickled cabbage.

The tedium of that winter, the spiritual disintegration of the many incarcerated men and the inhumanity of their guards, the cold, the lethargy and the despair – all those matters that reduced the prisoners to a state of inertia or an acute delirium caused by being driven beyond the limits of endurance – he omitted. He could not bring himself to speak of the hundreds he had met who had their spirits broken, their dreams smashed and their memories violated, and who were forced to work in freezing conditions though they were walking skeletons.

'It is no surprise that so little of the truth comes out,' he confessed finally. 'Some poor souls do not make it, but it is impossible to prove. The bodies are soaked in gasoline and burned in ditches.'

'What became of Private Watson?' someone asked in the ensuing silence.

Edward shrugged.

'And Private Fitzroy?'

There was another long hesitation. Edward tried to blot out the images.

'I'm afraid he didn't make it.'

The other men stared at him. Someone asked, 'And where are the others?'

'Watson is still in there.'

'And Stone? He has been listed by the enemy as one of their casualties.'

Edward frowned. 'He was unwell. I'm not sure what happened to him,' he replied. He glanced around the group and asked quietly, 'Have there been any letters for me?'

The Major shook his head. 'I'm not sure,' he said. 'Has it, Hartley?'

There was a sorrow in Edward's face and a long, pensive pause that weighed down on them all.

Then, as he stood up, out of the blue Hartley handed Edward something. He took the small pile of envelopes tentatively. A lump rose in his throat and he withdrew.

He recognized his mother's handwriting first and then the postcard from Harry, but in the halo of candlelight Alice's elegant handwriting, once so recognizable, looked unfamiliar. He noticed by the postmark that it was an old letter, written almost one year earlier, after he had left London.

He flipped an envelope over, studying it, feeling the closeness of the crisp silky paper. He put it to his nose, inhaling the sweet, intoxicating scent, and began to read.

Afterwards, as he tucked it under his pillow, a tide of disappointment flooded through him. She left the impression that the war had not altered her perceptions and outlook as it had transformed his own. He wanted to feel proud of her, but the truth was that she seemed consumed by her own concerns, rather than those of others. She did appear to yearn for him any more as he did her. She seemed more worried about her grandfather.

In his head he heard the screams, the groans and the wails of the dying men who had preserved their courage as they had dragged themselves in pain through the freezing mud as they forced their broken fingers into the soil and lay cold and hungry on their infested bunks. Silently he prayed for Peter Stone.

The second letter he opened was from a distressed Helga Coberg, who explained that her husband's Germanic name had become an insurmountable problem in London, even though neither she nor the Professor had any inclination to support Germany in the war. Furthermore, the Professor was not well and so they were moving to the countryside. Their old friend Jasper Lenz, who had received similar abuse and threats on account of his own connections with Austria, was alive and well and on leave. She let slip that he had been asked to become a translator for the British Government.. He had told them himself only the other evening. They had met him unexpectedly. He was having dinner in Soho with Alice.

Now, as Edward's mind turned to his wife, with her comfortable existence and the wilful liberties she took without any consideration for her reputation, his chest began to ache and grow heavy. His heart sank as he concluded, without any evidence, that it would be naive to think there was nothing going on between the.

He puffed out the candle and breathed its smokiness, a vast, irrational anger raging within him. How stupid he had been to ignore the anonymous warning he had received previously. A friend was their author – not an enemy.

Burying his head in the thin rough sack that served as his pillow, he closed his eyes, but sleep was futile. He remembered something Jasper had said to him at his wedding. 'You have a beautiful wife and you would be a wise man not to leave her,' he had said. Without hesitation, Edward jumped to the only conclusion he could think of. It could only mean one thing: Jasper was in love with Alice.

Lying in the darkness, Edward's imagination ran wild. He pictured Alice and Jasper laughing together, their slurred outline lit only by the morbid glow of his own ridiculous jealousy. He would decide in the morning whether to go to her and confront her, although it might be better for them all if she assumed him dead.

Chapter 3

Oblivious to the lies and misunderstandings that implicated her regarding Jasper, Alice's days passed, consumed by the anguish of patients and mundane chores. Every dawn she walked to work and each night she walked home under the heavy moon, listening to the sky's constant lulls and low, hollow thudding.

The irony was that her innocent friendship with Jasper meant nothing to her, but she was intoxicated by another opium. Whenever she found herself thinking of the handsome surgeon she had assisted in the operating theatre, she fought with herself, tending diligently to her patients, as if the influence of her encounter with the doctor had satiated something. It coursed feverishly through her veins, ravaging every sinew, making her soar.

But she knew it was forbidden and she had neither the courage nor conviction to meet with him, fearing that such an attempt would surely prove futile and even obliterate the feeling that existed, which was beautiful in its abstraction.

She could not avoid thinking of him, even as a raid began outside the hospital one day. It was the noise that woke her from her reverie. The sound rose and fell, its pulse ever-constant. It was the kettle whistling, the clock ticking, the passing of fate, the buzz of furious bees. She strained her head out of the window to try to get a better look, transfixed by the sun as it lit the cobwebs like telephone wires, but could see nothing except low clouds.

Most of the patients were incapable of moving, with limbs helplessly strung up or tied to inter-connecting tubes. Those who could leave their beds hid under them.

Shrapnel crashed and thundered upon the trees and buildings. Every time the sky cracked, boys, buckets, beds and bottles jumped like fallow deer with nowhere to hide. They were all of them at the mercy of a violent unseen force, fragile butterflies blown at the wind's whim.

Mr Pitts trembled and screamed, and Mr Fowler, who had never even fought in France, but had walked into the hospital one day with a sore on his leg, was up and dressed in his crumpled khaki uniform ready with his bayonet.

Hunched on the floor, knees tucked against her chest, Alice glanced around at the splints and thought how odd that they should become so familiar to the ward that they had become part of its furniture. She thought this, even as she was praying.

She could do nothing for Mr Pitts's pain. His reserve had broken, but his spotted handkerchief wasn't large enough to cover his startled face.

The silence, when it came at last, felt infinite, the tiny gap between the ending of a cadence and the beginning of the applause. War was full of noise, but it generated silence, and perhaps that was its most sinister quality.

'Will you give us something to help us sleep?' asked Mr Pitts. 'Them Zeppelin things give us nightmares.'

'Yes, Harold.' She wished she could have something too.

That day so many stretchers came in that they laid them on the floor in the hallway and in the kitchens and anywhere they could find a piece of hungry, pregnant floor waiting to be filled with the shouts and sweats of the newly injured. The carriers lined up outside and queued along the street.

'Naaaarse! Can I have another of those Marmite

sandwiches?' The voice cried out from behind the screen. 'Naaarse!' it called again more insistently.

Alice smoothed down her apron and pulled back the screen. Mr Flint lay on five or six pillows, held in position by tape and webbing passed under his arm and attached to the bedposts. He had lost both legs and one arm below the elbow. They didn't know if he would live.

His omelette was made with powdered eggs, but he didn't complain about its grainy texture or cloying taste. He seemed satisfied, though there was no more Marmite.

'He likes you.' Number 22, Mr Dickinson, seemed to have clocked everything.

'Will you have dinner with me when I get out?' said Mr Flint.

'I would love to,' said Alice. She knew how sick he was. She propped up the pillows and carried on with her duties.

Whenever a man died they took him away on a stretcher, just as he had come in, except with a flag draped over him. Every man who could do so rose to his feet as the covered stretcher left. Another empty stretcher was carried behind another screen further down. There was shuffle of feet as the men stood to attention, and when the orderlies came out again the folds of the flag had ballooned up to receive and embrace a man's body.

Laying trays helped to soothe her. She did forty-five that day, thirteen pieces on each one, which made five hundred and eighty-five altogether. Afterwards, she returned to the dispensary room and took out Edward's photograph. His eyes seemed to follow her, as if interrogating her. He must be dead, she told herself, and if he is, why shouldn't I be free?

After the encounter at the operating theatre she had not once caught sight of Sebastian Peterson. She wondered if he might have been posted somewhere else. That was until one afternoon at about four, when she was crossing the corridor. She was wearing her usual uniform and her apron needed changing. As she turned toward the staircase on her way to the staff room, Sebastian suddenly stood before her. He wore a white doctor's coat and stopped before Alice, an expression of happy surprise spreading across his face.

'How are you?'

Alice, somewhat startled, said nothing at first. She felt her heart throb. A few seconds of silence passed during which Sebastian gazed with admiration at her face.

She looked away, studying for no reason at all the box of bandages lying on the table, clutching her apron and twisting it involuntarily. Her cheeks flushed. She dared not look at him.

Peterson understood and tried to encourage Alice's eyes to meet his own.

'I was just going for some lunch. Would you like to join me?'

Alice stared at him. She wanted to answer, casually and cheerfully, that innocent suggestion of his that was in reality so loaded with meaning. She wanted to close herself to his words, to deny them of their significance and so shake off their significance, but she found herself speechless. She felt herself shiver.

The silence was a dizzying chasm.

'Well, I mustn't keep you any longer,' she said.

'Yes. I think I'm needed in Ward D,' said Alice, realizing immediately that she probably was and should not dally.

Quickly she ran up the staircase. At the top, she glanced down and caught a brief glimpse of the doctor's white coat. Her emotions were overwhelming. She felt suffocated.

There was something about this man, something inexplicable that affected and perturbed her by its strangeness. That face of his, with its noble, distinguished, odd beauty, produced in her a seismic reaction.

It was as if her soul was being ripped away by a force that she could not explain. She knew only that she was helpless in the face of it.

That night she wrestled with her tortured conscience. 'This is ridiculous,' she told herself. 'I am not free.' Then, as if gripped by the delirium of a fever, she added, 'Am I bound to Edward or am I not? Is he alive or is he dead? Why else would he have stopped writing to me? I have tried hard to be loyal to him, but have my faith and resolution been in vain? Am I being faithful – only – to a ghost?'

It was worrying to hear from Helga that her old friend Jasper, who she had met briefly for supper one evening, had returned to France. He had spoken of many terrible sights that he had witnessed, of huge craters caused by mines that had been exploded, men paralyzed by shock, slabs of concrete from shell-proof shelters hurled fifty or sixty yards, and of his horse that had needed to be put down.

An old letter arrived from Harry.

'Many thanks for the socks and the soap is a luxury. We are continuing with the advance. I had another man down last week. He was pulse-less for hours. Today he is eating tinned chicken soup and travels to the base with me tomorrow, with a healthy stump! It's incredible what can be achieved in the din and dust of the camp, and a good hot ration and sleep goes a long way.'

There was no news of Edward. The letter was dated 1915.

Then she received a letter from Marigold. She and her sister Violet were to visit Cheyne Walk.

For Edward's sake she greeted them warmly, and even Grandfather abandoned his books and welcomed the visitors with compassion.

Marigold, pale in her anxiety, concealed her fading hopes for her son with a chirpy, nervous laugh. Her sister Violet, an angular lady with a pointed chin and beady eyes, promptly addressed Alice as 'dear', which immediately caused irritation. As she spoke her eyes soaked up the young wife, the room and the furniture, without expressing any concern for Edward, as if searching for whatever items Edward might have brought with him with a view to reclaiming them.

Violet eyed Alice as if she knew exactly what this young woman had been up to during her long separation from Edward. Marigold nodded furiously at everything her sister said. Violet remained keen to know whether Alice remained in the habit of conducting sufficient enquiries as to Edward's whereabouts, whether she had consulted the appropriate officers and whether she had heard from any of his friends or acquaintances.

Tears of exasperation rose to Alice's eyes. The intense grilling felt so painful that she racked her brains for some pithy retort to fire back that would silence them. She decided upon reflection that the effort of losing her temper was unworthy. Instead, she nodded amicably, determining to drown them both with assurances and vowing to remain strong. With her black-and-white values and straightforward judgments, it seemed remarkable that the older generation, who were spectators to the war, should find it harder to cope than those who faced death and oblivion at first hand. Alice, having not had any children, underestimated the effect on the mature population of such relentless, dwindling hope.

Violet painted Edward's father as a powerful, well-connected man. Humphrey trained the officers; Humphrey knew the Prime Minister; Humphrey seemed to know the entire Houses of Parliament. Little by little, Alice received the impression that if Humphrey had been consulted, there would never have been a war.

'Tell me, Mother,' said Alice, interrupting Violet. 'Have you or your husband heard anything – *anything* at all – that would prove to us Edward is still alive?'

After a long pause Marigold uttered, rather enigmatically, 'My husband has heard nothing.' She blew her nose in to her handkerchief.

It was strange that not a snippet of news had been forthcoming from Edward's father, who must surely have been privy to even the most confidential information at the War Office. Overcome by indignation, Alice decided she would ask him herself.

Grandfather, who was standing at the window, turned around. He seemed in better spirits and his chest had cleared. The tonic he had been taking had made a difference. 'Won't you stay for supper?' he asked Marigold.

It was Violet who answered. 'Thank you, dear, but we are already late. Humphrey's friends, you know.'

Marigold's dull eyes suddenly sparkled at the distinguished and influential circles to which Humphrey would introduce her.

'What a shame,' replied Grandfather. There was something about this mother, with her clumsy manners and strained, enigmatic smile that unnerved him. He suspected that she knew more than she was saying, and yet the idea seemed absurd that if she had any news of what had happened to Edward she would not inform Alice.

Alice did not invite the women to return the following

day. Edward's loss could not be illuminated by discussion, and perhaps the tone of Violet's voice only made matters worse. Perhaps it was her gentleness that was most disturbing. It might have suggested to Alice that she deserved to be pitied, which she absolutely rejected.

When Marigold and Violet had left the long days at work continued and the torrents of Alice's conscience surged on. A letter to Edward's father brought the usual vague, polite reply. He promised to keep her posted so that when on St Patrick's Day the blue envelope fell on to the doormat, the thought crossed her mind that somehow he might have been personally responsible, before she realized he could not possibly have been.

She recognized Edward's handwriting immediately. Then she noticed the postmark. It was the letter he had written the day after he had been captured. It reached her now, almost sixteen months later.

'Do you love me? Are you missing me? That you are there for me is the one thought that binds me to life – that you are thinking of me and waiting for me.'

She read the letter through once again, but the words she had once so longed to hear felt disconnected.

At that instant someone tapped on the door. Grandfather poked his head around. He had recognized Edward's handwriting, and he was filled with impatience. 'Well?'

Alice passed him the sheet of thin pale-blue paper, her heart leaden. 'It's almost two years old,' she sighed. 'It proves nothing.'

Grasping it, Grandfather disappeared into his study. He lit a pipe and began to read. Afterwards he resolved it might be wiser to say and do nothing. But he remained sure that he was right about Marigold, though what secret she was holding remained uncertain.

Chapter 4

The gentlemen of the Fourteenth Reserve Battalion were waiting to receive their orders. It was still light and in the golden air snatches of shellfire popped and cracked in the distance at Zillebeke. A chill from the west whipped through the open gate, lifting hairs and forming goosebumps beneath the coarse woollen uniforms.

Following General Field's instructions, Edward's company had gathered in the yard beside Essex Farm, so that a group photograph could be taken. There were twelve of them in all, and especially for the occasion each man had shaved and combed his hair, so that everyone would look smart. They had been instructed to look cheerful, for a man who could appear strong in the face of adversity and in the presence of death was worth ten of the enemy. The reputation of the British army was held up by smiles.

Captain Talbot was seated in the middle of the group, for at fifty-three years old he was the most senior officer, and the unspoken elder among the men. Edward was happy to be back with his old Sergeant. Talbot had survived the attack at Lys and used his wits to evade capture. Sergeant Smith, the most considerate, had even brought a cushion, which consisted of a kit bag stuffed generously with socks.

Talbot, assuming his central position, folded his arms over his chest and adopted a confident, steely expression, without overtly grinning. Behind him, to the sides, stood

Winter. Edward, rifle flung over his shoulder, had assumed a blank, emotionless stare, his focus pinned to a bale of hay. He felt calm and rested. He had returned from his recent leave a new man and he had been promoted.

Winter shifted impatiently, alternating his weight from one leg to the other. Hands dangling at his sides, he continued fidgeting, while the photographer, a short, muscular Irishman whose job was to report the war, hopped and darted about in his efforts to arrange the group as if he was at a wedding.

'Move in, please, everyone,' he commanded, and the men shuffled sideways in opposite directions.

Hand on chin, he surveyed the group, most of whom had not yet fought in the trenches. He stroked his elegant moustache.

To the left of Captain Talbot sat Privates Leach, Dimple and Lemsford. Leach sported a pleasant yet stone-faced look. He was from Newport and had just arrived. Behind his fear and anxiety there was a steadfast quality and an unshakeable resolve that, even here on the periphery, he revealed to no one. Edward was of the view that Leach was a man who, if ever he should find himself injured, would not abandon his team. He seemed to anticipate the nightmare of the trenches and had prepared himself; it had nothing to do with his background, for he had worked on an estate, rearing pigs.

Dimple, who even within earshot of the most deafening shellfire never lost his nerve, was terrified of having his photograph taken. Standing awkwardly, he waited with a white face and trembling lip for the click of the camera, as if it were to be his last portrait. They all loved Dimple, so-called on account of his cherubic cheeks with their tiny dents, for the men had no doubt that in their hour of need Dimple would not crumble.

He was a God-fearing chap, immediately recognizable as a teenager by the fine parrot-down hair that grew upon his chin when he had not shaved. By his own admission, he had been the worst newspaper lad in England, although he had managed to sign up at sixteen after he lied about his age and education. Soon after his training, he found a sweetheart, and while on leave had married her.

Lemsford was a financial risk assessor in Bath. He was without doubt the scrawniest, puniest soldier in the British army, but concealed behind this weakling appearance a wealth of tolerance and experience. Unable to forget his profession even now as he contemplated the battlefield, as the photographer adjusted his lens, and what sum might be appropriate to insure their lives.

Next in line came Rutherford and Brown.

Destiny had brought Brown to them from St David's, where he was studying to be a vet. Rutherford was a butcher by trade, with his own flock of sheep. Leach and Brown cogitated about how, when it was all over, they might set up a business. All that was needed was a few acres of grazing pasture and Brown's superior expert medical knowledge.

Leach, who had a habit of conjuring grandiose schemes, pictured himself balding and pot-bellied, having written all about the war in his memoirs, surrounded by a hundred grandchildren.

Brown had begun his stint in the Artillery. There shone in this young soldier, with his pale green eyes, a passion. He explained to the men with enthusiasm and so bright a face that the war would not be won without the horses.

Privates Harris and Pickford remained neutral. Harris wrote anything that occurred in a diary and drew cartoons.

Pickford kept himself to himself.

One addition to the group without which it would not have been complete was a small black cat. Brown had discovered it hiding under a hedge and had lured it with some tinned spam into the vicinity of the barn. Judging by its rounded belly, it did very well off the scraps thrown by the soldiers. With no owner in sight, they christened it Victory, on account of the lofty, superior manner in which it held its head. After much debate, he took up his position, front paws neatly together, in front of Talbot.

Before the bulb flashed the photographer shouted, 'For England!' Proudly and defiantly, the soldiers looked directly at the camera. The photographer grasped the shutter and everyone remained still, each asking himself: 'Is this the last photograph ever to be taken of me?'

Afterwards, Edward drew the crumpled photograph of Alice from his pocket. He felt conflicted. He had no choice but to love those beautiful, soulful eyes and that intelligent, winning smile, but he was convinced that it was the face of an adulteress. He had thought long and hard whether to return to London to talk to her, but, despising confrontation, decided he would wait a while. He needed time.

Hours later, under camouflage of clouds pregnant with rain and so dark it might have been midnight, Edward and his regiment began to march. In the distance the offbeat rhythm of gunfire popped around the hillsides, but it did nothing to soothe Edward. As he trudged relentlessly toward his destiny, he could hear only the constant drumming of his thumping heart.

'Come on, chaps!' Occasionally someone would interrupt with a burst of encouragement.

There was no other sound in the communication trench, save for the squelching of boots in mud as they sank and came up again and the intermittent din of the firing. It sucked them down and then released them reluctantly, as if the very earth was dragging them, visceral and organic, to their sticky, doomed, inevitable fate.

War cheapens life until it has little value. Fate played pitch-and-toss with humanity. There was nothing to be done. If war was a drama, the feeling was it should be a musical comedy. Philosophy, culture, religion had lost their meaning. What mattered was: are you a good sport?

Occasionally someone ahead stopped, the line of men backed up and the entire march came to a halt. Standing helplessly in a zigzag of gloopy filth, he could see only the ghoulish stare of the gas mask clanking on Brown's saturated kit bag directly in front of him.

There was something else in the ebb and flow of this line that affected Edward. A dependency existed, borne of the slow, painful, rhythmic trudge and punctuated by irritated shouts of abuse when anyone fell or stopped – as if they were one long creature with a head, body and tail.

He felt in this rotting, reeking hole a sense of brotherhood for his fellows that went deeper than anything he might share with any woman. Each part depended on the other. It was different to anything he had experienced. The constancy of the men for each other, out of duty, was unbreakable. The harder the going, the more fiercely they ploughed on, as if nothing could divide them.

They arrived at Forest Ridge, took off their kit and waited for the mules to bring up the rations while the captain handed Talbot his gumboots and relieved him of duty. They fitted perfectly – the rotting, putrid cloths stuffed at the toe end ensured they would fit anyone.

The captain wished them luck, saluted and then he turned, hauling his sodden mud-caked bag on to his back, and walked off. The hope of respite seemed to dissipate about him, his uniform so covered with mud it might have been made of it.

Up at ground level, some of the men had carved sleeping holes into the trench sides. It was preferable to the hideous flood that lay beneath the surface. Edward's home was a hole in the third trench that might have been ten feet down. Although narrow, it fitted a bunk and a table, and he felt lucky to have it. There must have been almost twenty men further down in a space of thirty feet wide and five feet high. In the confusion of the deeper chambers men slept sitting upright, packed together with the stench of their unwashed bodies and the overflowing latrines.

Captain Talbot took the lower bunk. He stretched his legs and scratched his head. He had been here before. He was used to the lice and they no longer bothered him. 'When we get out, I'm going to write to Mr Lloyd George,' he said.

'What will you say?'

'I'm going to complain about the work conditions.'

For a moment their eyes met, glittering.

Edward unpacked some of the damp kit he had lugged with him: a soggy packet of cigarettes, a periscope, three bars of chocolate he had been given by Pierre Lapin's wife, and a bottle of whisky that no rain could spoil. At last he took out the green fountain pen and the postcard he had bought at Rouen. He slipped them into his inside breast pocket, next to the golden locket Alice had given him.

'And the interior décor could do with an overhaul,' he said, sitting down at the table and pulling across two glasses.

A few minutes later, still sitting in his chair, Talbot's exhausted body lay slumped forward. His head had dropped to his chest and the sound of his heavy snores struggling against the soaring thuds beyond the mud walls.

Private Brown emerged from the left as Edward came out from the dugout.

'How's Victory?'

'Left him with a villager. We could have done with him here!'

What he meant was they could have done with a rat catcher.

'Come and have a drink. Get the others.'

Dimple shuddered as the whisky went down. He didn't look old enough to drink, let alone be crawling around having been tasked with the job of planting explosives.

Brown, Lemsford and Leach smoked cigarettes, and Edward joined in. Winter had written on a piece of cardboard 'The Savoy Grill' and with a piece of string and two bits of wire somehow managed to fix the sign above the doorway of the dugout.

The men disappeared, back into the underground labyrinth city, with its lanes, alleys, crossroads and avenues, to the cave they now called home, lit by candles in bottles. All was foul-smelling and filth-ridden. The smoke felt suffocating, but it was nothing to the difficulty in breathing through a gas mask. Edward covered the sleeping Talbot with his oilskin, and, still unable to sleep, stuck his head outside the dugout. He couldn't be bothered to take the mask.

The sky was dark save for the brilliant circles of light bursting in waves. He preferred night to day duty. The four hours seemed to pass quickly. Teeth chattering, he waited for the dawn beside the swaying, creaking hurricane lamp dangling by the platform, Verey pistol in hand. As the half-rain, half-snow dabbed against the light, he watched the flakes stick and melt away. The ebbing descent of howitzers reminded him of timpani bursts, a dramatic conclusion to a dissonant symphony, the shattering of waves against cliff.

There was no chance of retrieving the bodies still out there in the field. No man's land was no more than a vast, unsheltered, gruesome grave. If you looked closely you could see where the sun had swelled up the dead with gas and turned them navy blue. They had dried like mummies, still frozen in their death positions, on their backs or bellies, sitting and kneeling. The crows pecked at their eyes and the maggots and rats gnawed at them.

Averting his eyes, he glanced eastwards and saw shells bursting in rapid succession at the foot of a promontory. Like a presaging storm the rumble increased. The bursts, previously distinct, blended in a white line of smoke.

Only two more weeks and he would be out for ten days, he thought to himself, and a sudden, inexplicable longing took hold of him to return to England. He felt dreadful. He bitterly regretted the letter to his parents regarding Alice. Naturally, they had written back immediately, without hesitation respecting his wishes. Now Alice was unaware that he was alive.

Having banished his wife from his thoughts, as the mist began to dissipate ahead, she flooded back into his mind with even more intensity. He could think only of her and how unfair he had been not to give her the opportunity to speak for herself. He felt gripped by desire for her and to be near her so that he might lay his head on her and be forgiven. Only she could wipe away his agony and desolation. He took his pen, unfolded the postcard and was still struggling to find the words to tell her he loved her, when Brown arrived to summon him for breakfast.

Chapter 5

Sitting in her nightgown before her dressing-table mirror, Alice noticed that her eyes had become encircled by deep shadows. Exhaustion and sadness were overpowering her.

Since Edward had gone life had changed beyond recognition. Meeting his relatives only served to reinforce the fact. Where once her days had been absorbed by giddy, stupid love and silly trifles, now they were subsumed in the clatter of cups and the shuffle of carpet slippers, of patients drained of everything except resignation.

Nowadays she lived among unmade beds and smashed and burnt limbs and torsos. When the ambulances arrived at the hospital the injured piled in. First of all came the walking wounded, who took the steaming mugs of coffee and tea that had been waiting. Men limped in with bandaged feet, some with only a nose and an eye showing. After that came the stretchers, which were left littered across the floor, while the gas lamps twisted overhead on their chains, contorting the shadows over the injured as if in judgment.

While the war seemed to be getting nowhere, the routine battle against time and mortality continued in London, just as oblivious to working hours, this one in a whirl of tourniquets, bandages, splints, gauze, peroxide eusol and saline, and another shift began. The bombs kept falling and the windows kept trembling, but by some miracle they did not shatter. Sometimes, while taking temperatures, a blind would suddenly blow and in the gap a glimpse of a black gulf crossed with bladed searchlights.

Then one afternoon she saw Sebastian Peterson. At first he didn't see her. He was striding towards the tuberculosis ward, stethoscope in hand. He looked purposeful.

Her heart banged so loudly that all her strength was needed to hush it; it was louder than the swish of a lame foot upon the stone floor and the soft tap of a rubber-tipped walking stick. Or the sound of her dull, fumbling fingers as she tidied the little rubber tubes in the trolley drawers. She moved on to the syringes, but even now she could still hear her heart beating. It was like a ticking bomb. It was as if she was standing on a precipice and a chasm had swung open. She stood there, torn between a man she had loved and assumed gone and a sense of something so remarkable it seemed death itself could not have prevented it. Everything felt divided, even the ward, half neat, orderly and crisp, the other half disordered khaki, boots, caps and mud.

Instead of the twenty-two lemons required for the recipe she squeezed the two she had into an old chipped jug and guessed the lemons.

Peterson was attending to number eight and several patients were waiting for him. At the risk of losing sight of him, she considered passing by whilst carrying the jug and pretending not to see him. But she stayed where she was. She had the overwhelming sense that an unavoidable destiny was presenting itself to her in the form of this man. Surrendering responsibility, she resolved to leave everything to chance.

'Nurse! Can I have some of that lemonade?' Alice tilted his head so that the straw met his mouth. The man lay on five or six pillows, held in position by tape and webbing passed under his arm and attached to the bedposts. He had lost both legs and one arm below the elbow. They didn't know if he would live.

'He likes you.' Number twenty-two nodded towards the bed where Peterson was hovering.

Alice ignored him. 'Drink up.'

'And you like him…' He managed to smile.

It struck her that men living so near to death were more aware of life than anyone.

After she had adjusted his pillows she put another blanket over him and tucked it into the corners. It was so cold in the ward that no one spoke. The silt on the electric lights was too thick and the fire smoked badly.

He soon fell asleep, lulled by his morphine.

Peterson, having finished with number twelve, folded his notes, looked absent-mindedly about him, and caught sight of Alice. He walked immediately over to her.

'I was wondering where I might find you,' he said, after they had stepped away from the beds.

'I'm usually here,' she said matter-of-factly.

'You must be due a break in that case. Would you like some tea? Or a walk, perhaps?'

Alice glanced at her watch, as if her decision depended on the hour. 'Why not.'

Wrapped in their overcoats, they set out and before long had reached the archway into the rose garden, which was empty.

'You know,' said Peterson, after they had been speaking for a while, the first time I saw you, I saw you as any man might see a pretty young woman. What you felt, what you thought of me and how I affected you – none of it mattered. In this dreadful war, I've come to realize nothing should be wasted. But, you see, I avoided the issue. I just gave up the idea of you because it would have been infamy. I saw you wearing a ring, and to trample over someone who cannot defend himself is a cowardice that I could never live with. If you were free and your husband was here I could take you from him with my bare fists, but, well, as it stands I have no one to fight.'

Alice stared at him, horrified by the directness of the words that yet filled her with admiration.

'It is impossible to know how to act.' He paused and as he stopped speaking the swirls of steam made by his words evaporated in the air.

Shivering, Alice gathered her blue coat around her. 'I have thought about it a great deal,' she said. 'For a long time I wondered if he had died, but now I am not sure...'

'But he has been missing in action for far longer than six months? As far as the War Office is concerned, Edward is dead. It doesn't any make sense.'

Alice looked away. She wanted to hide the look of alarm coupled with disbelief in her face. It seemed as if he had begun to doubt her sanity.

'It is true,' she said at last. She had almost forgotten Edward's parents entirely, but the mention of the War Office reminded her of her father-in-law. When she had asked him about the matter, he had promised to have the official papers sent from his office. But that was some months ago. Since then she had heard nothing. Now she recalled Edward's mother, and how Marigold had averted her eyes when asked about it, as if she did not wish to disclose what was passing through her mind and did not know what to say.

They turned by the bakery and watched the tram tracks gleaming on the hill like rivers.

'As I see it, you have a choice. At the moment you are

lost in your own no man's land. This not knowing, this state of doubt, or twilight, or whatever you want to call it, leaves you powerless. If your husband is still alive and has not contacted you, he has his reasons. If the war has taught us anything, it is that time is precious, and you should not waste it. Life is not meant to be a waiting game.'

Alice, who had neither the strength to object nor the courage, did not respond. Peterson was reading her, and she was in danger of losing herself.

A look of weariness showed in his eyes. 'I'm leaving next week,' he said. I am needed in Dieppe at the hospital. They are overwhelmed.'

They walked side by side without speaking. Alice filled the silence with her thoughts, because there were no words to express the dilemma she was facing. At last she held out her hand. 'I hope that our paths will cross again one day,' she said in a voice she tried to fill with courage.

She stood, like a fool, watching him go until the street lamps grew small. Her pale face blushed when she thought of the way he had looked at her.

On the way home she slipped into Harris's grocery shop, to buy a bottle of red wine under the counter, or 'the usual', as he liked to call it, to accompany Rose's potato soup. She did not want to return to Cheyne Walk. The apartment, still filled with her husband's belongings, seemed to represent a prolonged suffering. The sharpness of the pain intensified when she entertained the images of bliss and memories of happiness she had once known. These dreams tormented her and doubled her anguish. Still shaking from the cold, somewhere between exhilaration and agony, she walked the streets until she was warm and the blistering wind dried her damp eyes. She was alive, free and miserable.

Chapter 6

'Get the primus going!' Talbot sounded hoarse this morning. He'd been up for hours in the grey autumn drizzle.

Edward smiled. So far there had been a few stray shots, but little more. Already he had tramped the length of the narrow corridor between high sandbags. The air smelt of wet, dark, metallic clay and decaying bodies.

The men were yawning, standing in rows, with their bayonets fixed. Only Rutherford, Pickford and Harris had disappeared to collect their rations.

On slightly higher ground and eclipsing them from view was a large heap of rubble and, to the north, a lake, Zillebeke Bund. Nearby the men of the Royal Field Artillery had established their gun sites. The German trenches were at the top of the ridge just behind the long roll of barbed wire that stood like a wave, almost two hundred yards away. Directly ahead, a few paces in front, lay the forsaken trenches that were the grave of so many men who had held this part of the line in 1915.

Tonight, if the wind was with them, gas was going over from the front line immediately after stand-to. They were going to give the Hun a dose of his own medicine.

Talbot, all turned out in his mackintosh cape, stamped his feet to keep warm and stay awake.

'Where's Dimple?' he said.

'He's laying wires,' shouted back Brown from the duck walk.

'I think he's at the dump,' Winter, who was lighting the fire, corrected him.

That very instant a rat, fat-tailed and round-bellied, hopped from a sandbag and walked fearlessly along the parapet. It must have smelt the sweet, smoky intoxicating aroma of bacon, which Leach was frying over the small brazier down below.

'Lemsford! Where the devil are you?' Talbot yelled.

Private Lemsford was standing behind him. He had been loading the petrol tins on to the trolley to fetch water. There was still just enough for the *café-au-lait*, from the tin as usual, made with cocoa and powdered milk.

Edward looked around for Dimple, spotting him about twenty yards off surrounded by spades, picks and spare duck walks looking for flares. He was already exhausted having worked on the wiring all night.

Brown, who had seen the rat and let it go on unharmed, was getting ready to stand-to. He had already been on sentry in this position a few months back. He knew it well. He put on his overcoat over his equipment and cape and went round to the firing bay, taking his rifle out of the covered rack there before relieving Leach.

Although it was unwise to peer over the parapet during the day, with a periscope the German trenches were clearly visible. A penny glass in a metal clip fired on a stick would always attract the attention of an enemy soldier, and it worked wonders as a decoy. The trick was to raise it gradually. Then, as the glass shattered was as good a moment as any to sit on the platform with your back to the enemy. The real periscope could then be lifted atop a bayonet where it stood a far better chance against the snipers.

Right now hardly anything could be seen at all, only a faint line of earth and sandbags with the occasional pieces of timber dotted about, the whole like a mound of earth that had been thrown up by workmen excavating a drain. What had once been a wood was now a collection of stakes, like the broken teeth of some identifiable beast.

Eventually the word was passed from the next traverse to stand down, upon which all except Leach and a few others were free to get their breakfast.

Edward had no time to eat. He needed to write to Alice, but there was no time for that either. He had to do the duty rota, and there was an entire day's chores to organize and rifles to inspect.

'Charming life, isn't it...' called out Talbot, who was just coming out of the dugout as Edward was going in. 'Both sides bury themselves in mud holes and spy on each other through slits in the earth. Then they blow ten thousand pounds' worth of ammunition that hit no one and retire to their holes, like dogs after a fight.'

His nasal twang betrayed no emotion, but did not conceal his nerves, apparent in his darting, restless eyes and the slight tremor in hand.

Edward wanted to shake him by the hand and tell him, man to man, that nothing was going to go wrong. It was well known that life in the trenches could be without action. When you tired of sitting you could stand and glimpse between the sandbags, and if you were really bored you could fire a shot. But a man could be in a trench for a year and never fire a shot at all, since he might not have seen a Hun. At night there was more opportunity for firing. It kept a man awake to shoot from time to time and helped to while away the days. No wonder madness set in. There was a lot of time to think.

Talbot did not agree. 'Better the bombardments than death by boredom,' he quipped.

Edward cast back an uneasy smile. The lulls, such as they were, could make a man sentimental. He thought of Alice's open, beautiful face, of the lush rhythm of her desire that expressed her humanity.

After breakfast Harris, Winter and Rutherford formed a working party to improve the wire. Talbot allocated picks and shovels. Leach set about cleaning the wooden boards on the footway and Dimple slept, having been awake all night with no food.

The shelling died down as usual during the daytime and after the unrelenting night came the freezing cold. It was necessary to keep moving to stay warm. Edward, who had been continually on the lookout for signs of an attack after his adventure, made his way along towards the traverse to pick up his orders.

At a quarter past five the shelling resumed and it was against the intermittent crashes and thuds that Edward, having gone quite a distance, stumbled across gunners, stripped and sweating, each crew working like a machine. The swing and smack of the breechblock was as clean and sweet as a kiss, followed by a six-foot stream of crimson from the muzzle and a thunderclap of sound.

Back inside the trench, as they prepared to leave, every move was accompanied by the effort of muscles wrung with exhaustion.

'Come along!' Dimple, having not eaten anything, weak as a kitten, hardly made it along the endless duckboards.

'Where the hell have you been?' yelled Talbot, as Edward, breathless from his afternoon foray, took up his rifle and yanked on his helmet.

The moon was already out and the men, silhouetted in pairs at the top of the rise. Shots rang out. Some of the inky forms dropped. A plane was hit, like a broken butterfly spiralling to earth in a soft fluttering prelude to death.

More shots rang out. Somehow their luck held. Struggling over the crest they took cover in a shell hole. Harris carried Dimple's rifle for him.

Exhausted, one by one they crawled back into the dugout and drank tea. Each mug was sweetened with three spoons of sugar for energy. When the tea had gone down the mugs were topped up with whisky. At the top of their voices the men sang: 'Over there, over there... We'll be over, we're coming over... Send the word over there...'

Much later, by the light of a candle stub, a drowsy Edward and confused sobered himself up with a coffee. Propped up on his bunk, on his stomach, he began a letter to her. It was almost impossible to think straight behind the illusory protection afforded by the gas curtain that hung over the dugout entrance, but the urgent, desperate longing swelling in him suddenly took over. It was generated by the alchohol and the intensity of his predicament, together with an overwhelming feeling he had been too harsh in judging his wife. Perhaps she was not guilty after all. Maybe his injured pride had been the greatest casualty.

As the thick fountain pen nib dug into the thin paper, he recalled another letter he had once written to her, the time when he had tried to declare his love for her. Just like then, the words would not come. He found himself sorely regretting his mad, uncontrollable jealousy and what he had seen as Alice's disgrace. Nothing in the world could lighten his regret at what had happened, but he still had no proof. He had not heard from Jasper Lenz once. Nor had he been able to challenge him. Fortunately nothing had been said or done that he might have needed to take back, but there was more. Most crucially of all, he still loved her.

He burned with a new desire, his heart dazzled by her memory. He saw in this moment only the perfection of his love, bright as a fixed star, with no defects or flaws. He felt the soft, warm curves of her hips to the pillowy softness of her lips. He opened the gold locket that still contained a few strands of her golden hair. He breathed them in. He could even smell her delicate lily of the valley cologne.

'My beloved Alice, how can you ever forgive my strange, interminable silence? I am writing to you to let you know that I am safe and that I...'

At that instant a thunderous rumble shook the bowels of the dugout and a shower of earth smashed on to the table. The rumbling tore through the distance until the wave finally faded again.

A head appeared at the gas curtain.

'You all right, sir?'

'Yes, Winter.'

'Sir, there's a gunner here. Says he knows you.'

Edward looked up, pulled back the curtain and gasped. Black against the light, a man stood against mottling the shadows and a pair of sunken, enquiring eyes. They belonged to none other than Bombadier Hugh Coberg.

Chapter 7

At five o'clock William Purefoy sat down in his armchair and removed the spectacles from his nose when he was suddenly overcome by a strange, unfathomable sensation of weakness, a frailty more extreme than he had ever known. The feeling struck dread into him. He knew he didn't have long, but he had been counting on a few more months of summertime at least.

He looked at the calendar upon his desk. It was 6th July 1916.

Even an hour ago he had felt perfectly fine. He had been sitting in the chair reading *Punch*. Now, a cold sweat dampened his temple. He gazed at the window towards an invisible patch of green grass. He was finding it difficult to move. His legs, limp and heavy, had dragged him to the chair, and his arms felt quite numb. His body was failing.

He listened to the pattering of raindrops on the windowpane with pin-sharp clarity. His lungs wheezed and the air felt as if it was burning them. If only Alice was there with him, but she was at the hospital. He tried to call to Rose, but his voice would not reach; and then gradually he began to relax.

He saw his father, with his rumpled hair and long artistic fingers, digging the vegetable patch with his shovel, rhythmically casting the earth over his shoulder. And there was his mother in her red-and-white spotted apron, with her dark brown eyes that made half moons when she was happy. She was standing by the pantry in the sunlight as the dazzling rays glinted on the silvery tins of sardines and tomatoes and the honeyed jars of marmalade glowed amber. He noticed how their paper lids crackled and crunched as he touched them.

Now he was in the schoolyard, with its strawberry trees and their tiny bitter red fruit. Around him the other children were laughing and shouting at their hopscotch; he could smell the wet wool of their heavy duffle coats hanging on the hooks and touch their smooth toggles, gleaming by the gas lamp; he could see that little crack where the spider had gone in.

It was all so vivid.

Now he was sitting in the university lecture theatre, at the top looking down at the wide blackboard; he could hear the chalk scraping. The powdery dust choked him as it drew its filmy arcs.

The rest faded into a blur. His mind, disoriented, galloped ahead, hungry for more. But it could only skim the whole. Occasionally a small image burst to the surface like a water bubble, dispersing without any reference points.

Then everything became black and now, there he was, a pupil at 2 Brick Court chambers, with his dark suit and a wig so new he had to give it a good dusting with flour to make it look as if he had some experience, just like the older barristers. He could hear the clatter of carriages along Bird Cage Walk and smell the daffodils. Almost simultaneously he was seated in the corner of Simpsons eating kippers and drinking Earl Grey. He always had Earl Grey.

From there his mind leapt to the musty halls and great courtrooms where he had spent two rather long years of advocacy. He could breathe the dry, papery scent of old vellum that reeked of legal history.

If

That instant he saw Jennifer Tate, the gentle, slender girl who was to become his wife. How pretty she had been, with those cherry lips that curled upward at the edges and her shining auburn knot of hair and delicate earlobes. He remembered her making sandcastles with their beautiful daughter Isabelle.

Alice, with her shy, beautiful smile was holding that pink teddy bear he bought for her fourth birthday. She was counting to ten and he was hiding from her.

With an involuntary gasp, he saw her having given birth, lifeless, her nightdress bloodied and torn. Rose was leaning over and holding her hand. His chest wanted to heave. There was little Alice in her bright blue pinafore, now sitting on his lap clutching her baby blanket, now flinging her tiny arms around his neck and smelling of soap.

He started like a person emerging from a long, deep sleep to the convulsions of a violent earthquake. In those few brief seconds he saw his whole life summed up by one image, like a brief scene in a dream that brings together different events that would take years in the real world. He saw his darling granddaughter the way she truly was. She was his flesh and blood, but not as he was accustomed to seeing her. Never before had he seen her look so strong and calm. He had never noticed her poise, and her gentleness. Perhaps most amazing of all, he had never seen her face appear so graceful and serene, as if promising that everything would be fine.

As she came into his mind in this moment, with crystalline clarity, a tidal wave of love swept though him. What would become of her now that he was gone? The war had changed everything. How extraordinary were those flying machines and the telephone and the moving films… And Edward – would he ever return? And his work that was not finished yet… and his will, oh no, his will! He had forgotten where he had put it. Perhaps it was at the bottom of the filing cabinet, or in the bedroom…

All these thoughts whizzed through his mind one after the other, joining, separating and tumbling, churning higgledy-piggledy.

If only Alice was here.

What was that? It sounded like footsteps but he could not be sure. They sounded velvety, unreal eggshell steps. Perhaps he was dead already. No. It was definitely the rustle of shoes. Just like when his wife used to pad around the bedroom, so as not to wake him, although he was awake already. Ah! There she was. Or was she?

Alice had been concerned to see the light had faded in Grandfather's room but no lamp had been lit. She turned the brass handle of the door and, hearing it creak as usual, peered around the side.

'Grandfather? Are you there?'

When she saw him, her heart pounded harder. She turned on the lamp.

Grandfather lifted his hand, but almost immediately it dropped down again on to his lap.

'Alice?' he said faintly, his milky eyes unfocused, as if gazing into the spaces between the furniture.

'What can I get for you, Grandfather?' asked Alice, as she knelt down before him.

He wanted to respond, but his lips, now dry and white, would not move. Alice took her grandfather's hand and squeezed it, pressing her face into the now only slightly lifting chest.

'Grandfather?' Alice did not move an inch, as the hairs of the beard prickled upon her head. She knew what was happening. She saw death every day at the hospital, where its haunting shadow was a constant, but this was different. Here, where there were no ceremonial flags or military salutes, it didn't make it any easier – and this was not one of her patients, but her own grandfather, who she had loved unconditionally and who had taken care of her for as long as she could remember.

As she met his eyes the pain was so great she thought she would crumble. Her first reaction was to try to stop it happening, but almost immediately she knew that was pointless. How could one ever grow used to witnessing death, however, whenever or wherever it happened? The watcher was changed forever by it.

At the doorway she glimpsed Rose, her face crippled by alarm, cup her hand to her mouth and vanish. The faithful servant rushed to call for help, but it was hopeless.

William Purefoy sat in his armchair, surrounded by the objects that were dear to him – most of all, the thing he loved above all others, his granddaughter. Everyone else he had cared about was gone.

There was no sound save the drip-drip pulse of the rain upon the window and the occasional gentle exhaling of his breath. From time to time restrained sobs emanated from the adjacent room, an old servant's sobs, soft but persistent.

Any sense of fear had faded from William's eyes and the confusion had ebbed. Emptiness had replaced the previous flickerings of anxiety and alarm, and a stillness that did not belong to anywhere or anyone.

Alice, distraught, took her grandfather's hand and rested her head against the palm. It was cold and limp, and the manicured nails had turned pale. She lingered there, kneeling beside him, without a word, for how long it was impossible to say, until her schoolgirl's cheek came to rest on the lap. She was overwhelmed by loneliness. She was at the bottom of the sea. The fathoms of water weighed down above her, and she was drowning.

At the end of that indeterminate interval she felt a hand come to rest upon her shoulder. It belonged to a stranger. She did not know the name of the doctor who Rose had called, but, despite her confusion, she knew that it was not Peterson. The doctor fished the stethoscope from his leather bag and took a full, deep breath that seemed more like a sigh.

Alice glanced at him questioningly, and he shook his head. As he lowered the eyelids over Grandfather's staring eyes, she noticed something else. She had learned how it was commonplace for the faces of the dead, even in that fixed state, to subside into the long-lost expression of sleeping infancy; so tranquil and peaceful do they become that those who knew them might have said they were angels. There was an air of triumph in Grandfather's face.

The light had faded from the west. Alice, still sitting on the rug, did not stir from Grandfather's side. He was at the heart of her thoughts, as much as they were thoughts and the victory he had won had been instantaneous. Just hours ago he had been walking and speaking. The attack had come from somewhere unknown. There was no wound or operation, and this time the hole was in Alice, an eternal, boundless chasm that could and would never be filled again. There was no canvas screen, high enough to blot out a soldier's bandaged head, which could blot out the world.

Chapter 8

'Cheerio, Sanderson! This is all right!' Brown, on sentry, turned from his periscope to see Briggs disappear into the dugout. Driving rain lashed down on his already soaked-through uniform.

'It's bloody terrible, isn't it!' called back Edward as he climbed down a dozen steep slippery steps. Water ran down them but despite this Harris was sitting on the bottom.

The air below was hot and thick. The hollowed-out space was no more than six feet square and there were five of them. Talbot was checking kit; Winter and Dimple were sound asleep.

A lone figure stood beside the table in his mud-encrusted gunner's uniform, trousers torn at the thigh, elbow patched, gumboots smothered in slime.

Hugh gasped as Edward seized him by the shoulders, holding him in an iron grip so that he might get a better look at him. With eyelids stretched open, he stared at the lad as if he were a phantom.

'Can it really be you?' he gasped.

The gunner studied the thin, unkempt, unshaven officer before him, a widening grin spreading over his mud-smudged face. 'Edward!' he cried.

'How long have you been in Wipers?' Edward released him and he stepped back.

'I was sent here six weeks ago.' He fixed his eyes on Edward, mesmerized by how changed he was from the elegant, sharply dressed person he had met previously.

'How did you know I was here?' said Edward, still heady with surprise.

'Someone helping me with the electrics mentioned your name…'

'Winter?'

Hugh reached for the name that eluded him, his eyes lifting. 'Dimple, I think.'

Perhaps it was not so irregular that Hugh could have stumbled across Edward by chance. Artillerymen were often to be found along the trench lines laying wires and preparing targets. Hugh's new job was as a watcher.

Edward took out the rum and poured two glasses and Hugh drew a chair to the table and sat down opposite. The happy conversation went on for some time, but Hugh's conversation drifted away. He was in a kind of daze.

'Have you been home to London?' he asked.

'I have not had any leave,' said Edward, although it was not strictly true. He paused. 'Have you seen my wife?' he said, managing not to wince.

'Man to man, I have to tell you something, old chap. Alice has given up on you.' He regained his composure, leant over the table and whispered, 'She thinks you're dead.'

Edward lowered his head and sighed, 'Alice…' It was the first time in almost two years that he had heard the name spoken by another's lips. His eyes focused on his glass. He turned it in his fingers and the emotion contained so forcefully within him shook him violently. 'I wanted her to believe it. It's for the best.' He took a gulp.

'Good Lord. Why? What were we to think, any of us? Especially poor Alice?' He coughed several times, as if the words had become stuck in his throat. He told himself it was the rum.

Edward shot Hugh another long glance as if to say how complicated it all was, without actually explaining himself. Hugh was immature. It was unlikely, even if he did tell him, that he would understand. 'I did write,' he said at last. 'In the beginning.'

'So why did you stop?'

'I received an anonymous letter.'

Hugh took a gulp and coughed. He stared at the table, unable to look Edward in the eye. He had experienced many misgivings about sending that letter, even if he had done it out of love. Surely Alice deserved a better life than Edward could ever give her, a devoted husband who would love her as she deserved? He wanted the best for everyone. He wanted them all to be free.

An unsuspecting Edward continued, 'Anyway, my parents know that I'm alive. They are very loyal.'

'They kept your secret?' Hugh frowned. He wanted to tell Edward the truth, but it was impossible. Instead, protecting the mask of his innocence, he said. 'I have to tell you that my aunt believes Alice might be having an affair.'

Edward gave Hugh a moment's scrutiny. 'Come on then,' he said. 'What evidence do you have?'

Hugh, struggling with his own confused, conflicting emotions, looked Edward in the eye. 'I saw her with someone...' As he said it, the sound of a shell burst somewhere outside and obliterated the end of the sentence.

'So it is true...' Edward slammed down his mess tin in anger. He felt sick. He wanted to hit something. Hugh's word was the proof he had been seeking of his wife's infidelity.

Hugh had gone quiet. It seemed neither man wanted to discuss his feelings.

Edward felt the burning rum trickle at the back of his gullet, but it did nothing to soothe the earthquake ripping up his insides. Hugh had given him the proof he had been waiting for. He was a good sort and he had no reason to distrust his word. 'I managed to pop seven direct hits out of ten last week,' he said.

Almost as soon as it had begun the dreadful crashing of the sky subsided, but the evening's attacks had not yet begun in earnest. Up ahead, the mist over the ground had cleared a little. From time to time they could hear a Fritz whinnying, but most of the enemy were napping, curled up wherever they could find a spot.

'Have you heard from Harry?' asked Edward at last.

'I believe he is on fatigue,' replied Hugh. He scratched his neck. 'I'm on leave soon. You?'

At that moment Talbot, rasping, bitter-breathed, shouted down from the platform. 'The attack will be at 6.15!'

'Not sure,' said Edward as he followed Hugh outside and the two old friends shook hands.

'Look,' said Hugh casually, as he began off along the duck way, 'I don't want to speak out of turn, but...' He paused, as if struggling for the words. 'What I mean is, don't look back! Life is short. Everyone loves a beautiful woman.'

Hugh had already turned his back and was making his way off. Edward was left wondering what he meant.

He carried out his patrol that evening with a distracted diligence, only half-aware of the light tear shells as they sailed through the air. The shells burst with little noise and seemed to fade. The sickly sweet smell made his eyes dewy and the smell of pear drops lingered in his nostrils.

From the platform he could not see much, except the thorny network of barbed wire. He stared with wide eyes into the bleached, torn-up distance, thinking of Alice. What could Hugh have possibly meant?

A knife tore into his soul, forming a malignant, festering wound. Bereft, his despair flipped to fury at the idea that Alice had been unfaithful. His head swam and his heart froze. Images whirled round his head like dry, windblown leaves. If Alice had died it would have been easier to bear, but to die here in this hell with the knowledge she was in love with another man, devouring him with her adoring, kind eyes. That was such an agonizing thought that there was no way he could see himself living.

The obliqueness of Hugh's comment made him furious. Who could this other man who had wronged him be other than Jasper Lenz? One by one the primary suspects flashed through his head, but the name that kept coming back was Jasper.

'I'll murder him!' he said out loud, fist clenched around his revolver, pacing up and down the narrow alley of the trench as if it were a dark prison from which he would never escape.

'Sanderson!' The Captain was standing in front of him. He had a chit in his hand, which he read by the gold light. 'We need five men to bring in a German prisoner, dead or alive. And I'm afraid it's your turn.'

Orders were orders, even when it came to overt invitations to suicide. Did the Colonel know that the Sergeant went out with two men three hours ago and has not returned?

The Captain nodded.

The mere receipt of such an order felt like an insult. Sick at heart, Edward got ready with the others. Coffee was brewed and brandy slipped into water bottles. Haunted figures gathered around the tiny stove. The men could hear the bombardment starting up outside. Heavy howitzers shot first. Then the German artillery fire, previously intermittent, began to intensify. Someone was muttering the Hail Mary. It was Leach, who wasn't terribly religious, but who remembered the words and was reciting them off pat as if to take his mind off the situation.

Harris sat on the fire step, hands wrapped around his rifle so tightly that it would never drop. Talbot offered him his hip flask, but Harris could not remove his hand to take it.

Magazines were charged to the full, one round in the breech. Bayonets were examined to see if they slipped out of the scabbard silently. Revolvers were nicely oiled, all superfluous pieces of equipment discarded.

Towards five the guns went quiet. Both sides were saving shells for later, but the larks were singing louder than ever. There was some respite with the rain, which earlier had seemed so unrelenting, but now as dusk descended the sky cleared and the full moon made dark the shadows of the trenches.

Edward followed with the others down a disused forward sap, creeping in the shadows, rifle in hand, not knowing what might be lurking around the corner. The gunfire was deafening, its cruel decibels soared higher and higher. Suddenly, out of the left, came a whistle, Seconds later it was replied to by another, this one ahead to the right. They waited. The signal came again. Too late, they had been seen. It was a kaleidoscope of fool's errors

On the whistle Edward and the others stepped up. Though the murk he traced them, as each clambered towards their objective. Ahead, flashes lit up the hill, butted and broken with flesh and blood.

It was difficult to see what was happening with the rattling, jolting, shouting, the screams of the wounded, the roaring of shells and of mud flying everywhere. Line after line disappeared into the smoke. Up the ladders and over the parapets they streamed, as one or two wounded crawled back slowly.

To his left he glimpsed Brown and Winter out front, Rutherford and Harris. The others had vanished. Talbot, some way off, was yelling. As the sky darkened Edward heard: 'Come on, lads!' He recognized Pickford's voice, and at that moment saw Winter's body dancing with bullets.

The sky was pure noise, an unrelenting symphony of terror, through which the steady, rhythmic beat of human flesh was pounding.

After the thundering crescendo there was nothing, just white fog and the offbeat popping of a few rifles. There was no movement from the green and scarlet carpet of bodies. They lay without a sound, as if sleeping, and as if hewn organically from the ground.

Brown was sobbing and wailing like a baby. Dimple was bent over him.

With a fire swelling inside his chest and an agony he had not known, Edward charged forward. His cheeks were hot with salted tears.

He told himself he felt nothing as he covered the pitted land with his boots, inch by inch.

Ahead, in lumps and pieces, the line of green had fallen in an ocean wave. Behind him, following, hunched like fish hooks, another line was following. About twenty yards off Edward thought he glimpsed Rutherford, but it was difficult to say. His ears sang. The screech of his own gunfire had deadened them.

Talbot had been shot thrice, once in the leg and twice

in the chest. Brown helped, but Talbot was beyond hope. Lemsford was not responding. Edward picked him up and pulled him back to the trench, then went out again with a patrol to search for the missing. Poor Lemsford and one other unidentified could plainly be seen tangled in a heap among the German wire right under their parapet. Edward found the Boche wire uncut and pulled it apart with his bare hands. It was too late.

In the conflagration of khaki, the limbs of men jerked and jumped, but Edward's bones and muscles were still. He had reached the hill and the mound of spent humanity that waited for him there. He lay face up. Some inexplicable force had planted him there. Above him shrapnel blasted its jagged spikes into the air spaces not occupied by the noise. He noticed that his helmet was missing and wondered where he had lost it.

Details became magnified – a candle flame flickering in the light blue, a blackbird's song, a flint in a crack. Then, and only then, the faces; they belonged to those who had not yet properly known life, yet who knew they were on the brink of death. One, missing arms and legs, murmured in monotones. It sounded like a prayer, but nothing was divine any more. From every side, men pressed on into the oblivion. What was this visceral, unflinching duty that drove them on into the bowels of hell? What so-called just and decent cause could be so important to make this unspeakable, foul, depraved racket of suffering quiet again?

He could not feel his body. He could smell burning meat and chemicals. Around him, as the low, groaning moans subsided, for a split second he thought he heard singing. He gazed at the circling above him, but he could not tell if the spirals were birds or weapons. He watched the cloud run. That was the last thing he saw.

PART IV
1917–1918

Chapter 1

Cocooned in his green overcoat, Edward cut a solitary figure. It was four in the afternoon and a blistering sun glistened in the sky, but the breeze was brusque. As he lay there in the cane chair, he thought he could see the shimmer of a floating moon. Or perhaps it was the figment of a dream, like the silvery ball that hung on the Christmas tree, or the necklace he had tried to catch on his mother's neck when he had been a small child.

He smiled, allowing the faint warmth in the air to flow on to his face, sank back into the cushion. Fairy-floss clumps of apple blossom hung on the bough above his head and the scent of the flowers lingered in his nostrils. Spring had arrived early and was quite beautiful.

It felt exhilarating to be out of the trenches, like being born again. He wanted to cheer and shout. He wanted to lie down in the fresh grass and be swallowed by it.

At first, when he looked back, all he could identify was a great nothingness. In the blue light of his dreams he had seen Brown's frightened face, upturned at the skylarks as he dropped, heard Smith's screams and Rutherford's swearing as they dragged Brown back to the parapet; he smelt earth and blood and smoke and saw the gleaming red of Pickford's skull.

The last thing he remembered about Talbot was when he had been ahead, moving in slow motion towards the wire. Then he saw him as he had been before the attack, swigging rum when they had shared a drink that first day in the dugout.

Harris's limbs were in pieces as they hauled him along on the burlap sack. The noise, deafening the ears with its infernal instruments blanked out the shock of seeing what had happened to him.

Edward couldn't remember what had happened to Leach, Winter, Brown or any of the others. All he could see was a vast expanse, stripped of nature, pitted and cracked with shell craters.

The warmth of the sun had returned to Edward's cheeks and he felt the sunlight flicker over his hand, but that wretched, sickly-sweet smell of the battlefield was catching in his throat again.

When he closed his eyes death surrounded him in every permutation – blasted, vaporized, mutilated. He told himself all these forms meant nothing to their former owners and bore no connection with them. The exact moment when he had received his own wound was still missing. He could feel the dent in the right hand side of his forehead, but that was all.

Nothing he had witnessed, nothing he had imagined or dreaded could have prepared him for the shape and scale of what he had seen. Neither side had seemed able to advance over the broken, shattered ground. What did both have to show for it, other than the thousands of lost young lives?

Propped up in the chair, his thoughts drifted on, his butterfly head flitting from one unspeakable image to another. In his faraway eyes lay the lingering ghosts of yesterday with all their fear, sorrow and anger. At last, with a jolt, he came to his senses and shut the disobedient, persistent memory of Alice's face out of his head. There. He slammed it against the darkness.

It was as if a vast shutter had descended, wiping all trace of his former life and burying his emotional trauma. As long as the long summer evenings were warm there was a surprisingly acceptable piano in the common room to help him forget and his parents had been so supportive. He had written to them twice. He had told them everything that Hugh had told him.

After a few weeks the skin on the visible wounds on his right side and left leg had knitted and the flesh ached and throbbed less, but the invisible chasms of his heart had proved to be more complex fractures. Morphine's slumber could blot out the bitterness hidden in his soul, but it could never disperse it. It only forced the anger deeper.

Having banished it, he dwelt on positives, feeling how lucky he was to have been recovering here at the neurological centre near Amiens for two months. The French Red Cross nurses were very kind, although they spoke little English and he didn't always understand what they were trying to tell him. Persevering with his French, he asked questions, faltering on genders of nouns, but with such a musical ear that before long he might have been mistaken for a native. Phrasing each clause to perfection, his nasals and gutturals chimed with such fluidity that not one of them questioned where he lived or came from, though they could never quite place his accent.

At night, in the warm, comfortable bed he slept for hours and he was lucky enough to have a window that looked out across the rooftops. He could even see the cathedral, that very same edifice under whose earthly wings he had once hidden in fear of his life.

They were a mixed bunch of sick and wounded, mostly French and British. On the face of it they had little in common, but nightmares and wounds formed bonds beyond words. Most were in a state. A thousand disturbing thoughts occupied their minds, conflicting and confusing them. Lieutenant Fournier, having fought at Marne, had uncontrollable jerking and shaking in his legs. Bentley, from Sussex, suffered from what he called rational anxiety. The nervous breakdown made him delusional. He cowered behind a mulberry bush, firing with his arm at a small clump of willows, convinced that the Germans were hiding there.

For Edward there was not one who he would consider to be a friend. He recalled those he might call his best friends as ghosts, soft-edged and half-glimpsed, lurking in the shadows with other, unmentionable phantoms too awful to describe, close up and jumbled, racing in his head, tumbling one after the other.

Each evening those who could do so sat around a polished wooden table with weary spirits, tortured by homesickness. Edward came to dread these suppers. The sleep-inducing recollections of happy times before the war, the anecdotes and the trivia of their lives were recounted to each other ad nauseam. How he had yawned so that his jaws were threatened with dislocation at the tear-jerking tales of wives sorely missed who were paragons of virtue.

Their sickly yearning for home life made Edward feel he had to escape. And no one wanted to hear about schoolboy pranks, just as they would shut their ears to Edward's misty-eyed recollection of his youthful performance of Bach's 'Violin Concerto in A Major', if he had ever mentioned it.

In time he was persuaded to impart a little of his own story, but even then offered only scant, irrelevant information, such as musical pieces he had once played on his violin or places he had been, but never offering any information about his marriage. In obliterating the detail, he managed somehow to persuade himself that he could live without Alice. At least that was what he told himself, because he had long since convinced himself of her infidelity and his sensitive heart was still unable to forgive her.

It was June before he had recovered enough from his side wound to take trips into the centre of Amiens. There was no need to take a train from where he was in Longeau. Any vehicle served to give a soldier a life and an empty French ambulance served as a fine bus.

With a cheery smile the driver left him in the rue du Hocquet and from there he found his bearings. The poplars along the banks of the Somme were beginning to turn brown. From time to time cold gusts of wind disturbed the heavy boughs, but the leaves had not yet curled and turned inwards.

Amiens showed few signs of its previous occupation, with the odd crumbling wall or façade blacked by gunfire. There were no bombardments and the 8 o'clock curfew had been lifted. Some businesses appeared to be shut, but the jewellers and restaurants were doing a roaring trade and there was a long queue for a haircut. In select establishments it was possible to feast on boiled fillet of place or lobster with oyster and mushroom sauce, or to go to the pictures, or to take afternoon tea – and the brothels were thriving. All men sought comfort, just as all sought to be significant. It was what united them.

Edward, as he made his way from the Parc de l'Evèche, told himself he was not interested in cheap, disposable love – or any love, for that matter. He retraced his steps from 1915 and ended up at the Place de Gambetta.

Ahead, the great Cathedrale Notre-Dame glistened

against the dark clouds in the sky. How different it seemed to when he had hidden there with Fitzroy. With its vast flying buttresses and stabbing spire, it rose like an immense kindly guardian surveying all the chaos and heartache of humanity.

He would gladly have died to save this glorious edifice from destruction, but even the carved angels that promised to protect the building could defend it from the onslaught of war. On all sides sandbags had been piled high. One of the stained glass windows had been blown out and there were sections missing.

In his civilian clothes, hand upon the wooden stick that supported his intrepid, cautious approach, Edward approached the steps, remembering Fitzroy with a piercing sadness.

He proceeded to the south door, pausing often, still aching from the shrapnel that cut into his rib that had been too deep to be dug out. Once inside, he leant against the pillar, and listened.

A profound stillness filled the cavernous, echoing space. He was standing in the ambulatory, behind the altar, admiring its serene beauty of the Weeping Angel, when he was reminded of something else. Without warning the memory crept up on him. He grasped the stone slab for support. He saw the man quite vividly, dangling from the wire, scarecrow-like, eyes staring. He heard the shellfire as if he was back there and it was happening all over again, his gumboots sinking deep into the filth of the battlefield. The mud sucked him down. He was drowning in it. He recognized its bitter rancour.

When he came to his senses he felt the sweat on the back of his neck. He heard himself breathing. What might it be like to live a life without such recollections? That, he thought, would be a freedom really worth fighting for.

He gazed up at the decapitated martyrs of stone. Now they served only to remind him of the battlefield.

Suddenly he heard music. The choir was singing; the mass must have started. Glancing around, he noted how many women praying in the wide, open nave were dressed in the black clothes of mourning. It was hard not to wonder how many of their men had been killed or captured.

As he looked up at the wide, arching ceiling above the crossing, he was not thinking of those women and he was certainly not thinking of Alice. He was imagining the girl that had been drawing at the back of the nave that day he was here with Fitzroy and how, when the service had ended, outside he had seen her dark green beret floating in the crowd.

Last Sunday he had spotted her again, right there in the Chapelle d'Hiver, and yesterday, when he had been walking through the Portail de la Vierge. That time there had been no one about apart from a nun, deep in prayer, hands clasped, as if pleading for an end to this never-ending conflict.

Today he had not long to wait in the glow of the rose window when the same girl walked past him, sketchbook under arm. This had an electrifying effect on him, even though he saw nothing of her beautiful, mysterious eyes, with their curious languid sadness. She was elegantly dressed and glided effortlessly and gracefully.

Perhaps she thought him a pest and misunderstood his intentions. Or maybe she thought that he was just another foreign soldier looking for lazy love and nights of madness, drunk with urgency. In fact, he just wanted to talk to her. He missed the company of women.

Exhausted, he loitered at the front portico, studying an onion that had fallen from a street vendor's bicycle into the gutter. The translucent rays, shimmery gold in the summer evening, painted a light sheen upon the silky skin.

Kicking it with his foot, he wondered how much longer the girl would linger. Perhaps she had slipped out through the southern door. He peeped inside. There she was, still sitting there, as if testing him.

Ten minutes went by before, in a whirlwind warmer than the breeze, she whisked straight past him again. There was not a hint of a glance in his direction. Could she be ignoring him deliberately? It seemed unlikely that she had not seen him.

The girl hurried on, in a swirl of cotton flowers and lavender, still clutching her leather-bound sketchbook. Edward followed behind as she crossed over the canal on the Becouet Bridge and halted at a small traditional Amienoise. Before opening the black front door she turned and glanced around, as if she might have known he was pursuing her and was searching for him. Then she was gone. Edward, who was concentrating so hard he had entirely forgotten to lean on his walking stick, stood for a few moments. As he turned and walked away, he no longer saw the town as he had before. Everything had the freshness breathed back into it, the houses, restaurants, trees, and Edward himself.

Chapter 2

Alice glanced in the hallway mirror. Her cotton dress was starched and her shoes polished. It felt strange not to be wearing her uniform, but she was ready for whatever the day would throw at her. Only a thin black ribbon tied discreetly about her wrist gave any hint that she remained in mourning.

While the nation was preoccupied by its demand for freedom, Alice determined it was time to get away. She had left Grandfather's possessions exactly as they were in the apartment. Only the papers had been tidied. She had gathered them all up and put them, together with all the memories, creased and crumpled, into the drawer, so that one day, when she was wiser, she could retrieve them.

In her mind she saw him in his Chesterfield captain's chair, pipe in hand, fountain pen scratching away in the other. The scent of Earl Grey tea mingling with tobacco still lingered, and coats and hats hung on the hooks in the hallway, never to be retrieved by their former owners.

She closed the front door behind her and, pausing momentarily at the landing, glanced at the other one at the end of the corridor and the brass knocker in the shape of a fox. She could feel the swell of her heart against her chest and a light pulse in the flesh of her throat. She was remembering her friend Evie, and a song they had once sung together. Now there was only silence. An inconsolable sadness seemed to echo around the cold, empty walls. Alice saw people every day, but it was not hard to feel lonely. She had written to her in-laws to tell them about Grandfather, but there had been no letters from Marigold for months. News of Harry arrived only through Kitty; and Alice had not heard from Jasper since July. The one letter she had received was from Sebastian. 'I cannot find the words to tell you how much I feel for your loss, but it is unbearable to think that you have abandoned yourself to grief.'

Adept as she was in the art of pretending, she could not wholly conceal the profound effect that those forthright words had exerted on her, and as she began resolutely down the staircase without looking back, Alice felt like a fugitive from her past, but she did not admit the truth, which was that she was a fugitive from herself.

As the first rays of the rising sun could be seen, she arrived at Euston. Hours later London was behind her and the confusion of her private battles. Her destination was the Scottish fishing town of Nairn where she had lived as a child. By the middle of June the afternoons had become as calm and dozy as London in July. Sometimes during the sunny summer evenings an orchestra played to the few onlookers who were lucky enough to have wandered along the dunes of the East Beach. At these casual al fresco events traditional ballads and rousing marches were played and lilting harmonies that might have stirred any battle-weary troops into action.

It was a pleasure to tread between the humped sand hills. Loose stones grated and crunched beneath her sandals. Maidenhair fern and pink campion sprouted in the crevices between the rocks. Clover carpeted the barren patches and the sea glittered like spun silk. She could feel the grit between her toes and she could hear the music clearly. She breathed the fresh salt air, exhaling slowly like a sigh. It was a bright, breezy day and the wind made patterns on the surface of the water as it swirled and brushed the top of the grasses on the sloping dunes. She watched it pick up a stray sheet from one of the music stands, whisking it away until it fluttered down, leaf-like upon the waves.

Alice stopped and listened. If she strained her ears she could make out the deep, resonant tones of cellos and the rich harmony of violas. A solo violin began to wheel and soar above the strings, the reedy note weaving and twisting. She was thinking about Edward and whether she was free. She had not received any death certificate.

The track grew wider and snaked downwards. It felt like a miracle that a scarlet vetch could grow from such a poor shallow soil and provide such beauty. She might so easily have been tricked into the delusion that the world was not falling apart.

The headline that morning in the newspaper read 'Kitchener and staff perish at sea: lost on cruiser, perhaps torpedoed; England suspects spies of the deed'. She wondered if Kitchener was not dead at all. Rumour was it that he had escaped to Russia and that from there he was masterminding an attack that would bring victory.

Turning from the coastal path, she strolled on towards the orchard. Thistledown, powdery and white as fresh snow, grew about the hillside. High above a red kite glided effortlessly towards the hills, a fragile silhouette against the pale indigo sky.

This was the wild, free landscape of her youth. Over there, surrounded by mauve heather, was the ancient oak and the gnarled, twisted hollow where she hid as a child; and there, in the other direction, were the bluebells, buried like jewels in the spongy grasses where she once lay face up, awe-filled, gazing at the passing starlings. She smelt the green air and remembered the waft of celery and pine needles on her father's breath as he had once bent down to kiss her forehead. She had been about four years old.

The spring flowers seemed to mitigate the violence of her conscience, littered with the debris of events and feelings that had shattered any sheltered idyll. Gold oxalis and wild marigolds mingled with the silvery peach of asphodels in secret glades where hairy-footed flower bees feasted on lungwort.

It was as if there were two versions of herself. One was the Alice who had gone to Victoria Station with Edward and bidden him farewell; that frail, weak, bewildered young woman of twenty-three who stood in the steam among the tracks, waving at the receding clatter of the train's wheels. Back then, swathed in naivety, at least she had felt she understood something that validated her existence. The burgeoning of arrogance and the heady joy of her senses had created an impression of fulfillment.

The other Alice was the one who had somehow pulled herself together, whose very spirit had been transformed by the agony of others. The older, pragmatic Alice was more cynical. She had little in common with her former self, with which she coped uncomfortably.

Pausing in the shade of the ancient yew, she shook out the sand from her shoe. The haunting music floated on the breeze, deposited like a gift into her ears. It was languid and slow, and felt eternal and comforting, so bright that it might have eclipsed any memory of a war. She picked one of the buttercups clustering on the ground and put it to her chin.

If only Edward could have been there to hear it. The buttercup twirled between thumb and forefinger as she tried to picture him, but all she could see was his shadow, a willowy outline.

From the little wooden bridge she carried along towards the apple orchard, glimpsing the swing where she had often sat reading. She could see her father, imagine him pushing her gently. As she recalled the shapes and scents of his protection, she saw her grandfather, tasted the ice-cream he bought for her, a complicated jigsaw puzzle they once did together.

While the high notes continued to pierce and hang on the air, her imagination began to bleed more memories, of the soldiers in the hospital with their visible and invisible scars. Perhaps it was better that Edward had died than suffer like one of those poor souls.

In the meadow a pale butterfly flapped its wings on a cornflower. A figure climbed down from the wooden stile, smiled and waved. She scarcely recognized the pretty young girl in the light pink coat that clung to her outline and revealed her pregnancy. Alice nodded and waved back. She couldn't help wondering what her own fate might have been if Edward had given her a child, as she had once imagined.

How many more innocent lives would this relentless monster continue to wreck on both sides? How many more lovers would it tear apart and how many innocent children would suffer because it had stolen the futures of so many people? How many more hearts were still to be broken on its merciless, senseless account? If there should be any good to come out of it at all, it would take a lifetime to fathom.

The orchard was just as she remembered. Barlett pears dangled on droopy branches and Pippins clustered in friendly lumps for as far as the eye could see. She picked one up, bit into its bittersweet flesh from the ground. The cruel crisis of conscience that had tortured her previously began to intensify. The strange, meandering landscape of her independence was beginning to pall, while the future seemed vast and unknown, a lonely, deserted territory. Was she destined to travel it on her own?

The air had grown cold and her skin prickled with fine hairs that stood to attention. The larks began to sing, their voices rising and falling in waterfall cascades of varying resonance, effortlessly drifting in the direction of the huge red sun.

She watched the dear, slight figure, bent by age, come into view and the arm slowly lift as she signalled.

Rose waved cheerfully and Alice waved back.

There was a comforting familiarity to the cottage. She loved staying there because it reminded her of better times. The wooden swing with the crack on the seat was just the same as when she had first sat on it aged four years old. The yellow wallpaper had not changed; nor had the flagstone floor with its uneven ripples and familiar cracks.

A card had arrived from Harry Lloyd. He was on leave but there was not enough time for him to wait until she got back. She was saddened at the thought that she would miss him.

Less than an hour later she was sitting at the kitchen table and Rose was crouching mechanically over the stove that stood in the corner with a faraway look in her eyes. Perhaps she was painting in her mind a child or picturing the mutual friends and acquaintances the war had stolen from them. Perhaps she had an admirer.

Rose laughed at the suggestion.

Alice recalled the tones of that clear, high laugh. In her mind she conjured a thousand smiles and turns of thought and speech, as if she recalled not just her friend, the housekeeper, but all those she knew who had died fighting.

Now Rose had drawn a stool to the table and was sitting beside Alice, who had hardly touched the soup of vegetables, which were fresh from the garden. 'What's wrong?' she asked the girl she loved as a daughter.

'Nothing,' replied Alice, dipping her spoon into the bowl and stirring. How could she eat?

'It's not nothing,' said Rose. 'Why not write it down?'

Alice smiled.

Rose had reminded her of the diary she had written, the one she had left behind, together with all the heartache that was engraved in its pages. Now she wanted to write another story – one without the waiting, the suspense and the mourning. She tried to explain, but the words seemed to jumble.

A tear glistened in the soft blue eye, and Rose looked disbelievingly at her. Adjusting her mop of white hair with her fingers, she said, 'Alice, you forget that I have known you since you were a wee thing.'

'And have I disappointed you?' asked Alice. A scarcely imperceptible shadow of sorrow crossed her face, as if she were regretting the lie she had blurted out, the one about not wanting ever to love again.

Their glances locked. Alice struggled to cast off the enquiry of that expression that stabbed her very soul, but to no avail.

'Edward let you go long ago,' said Rose at last. 'The time has come for you to finally let *him* go.'

Rose took her hand. It was a comforting gesture, and one that seemed to replace the need for words. How expertly she recalled those long-gone years, spent filling the mind of her adopted child with stores of knowledge and becoming attached to her as her nature developed. How she remembered tracing in this girl traits of her old friends Jennifer and William Purefoy, who awakened in her own heart both melancholy and joy.

'Now more than ever love is our only grace. It should be given and received freely.'

An overwhelmed Alice replied, 'I never wanted to disappoint you. Or anyone.'

'Oh, my dear child, you could never do that,' said Rose. 'Good night.' She walked from the kitchen humming.

In the sanctuary of her bedroom Alice sat down at her dressing table. She brushed her hair mechanically, noticing long white hairs entangled in the bristles. As she threaded it into its usual plait, she felt how much thinner and lighter it had become, as if in that one single aspect of her lay all the withering, slow, intangible frailness of lost time.

Awake and unable to sleep, she curled in the armchair, knees up, watching the little sailing boats bobbing like seagulls and listening to the waves skimming the shore in their soft reassuring rhythms. A doubt twisted and stretched inside her. The mixture of depression and exhilaration was disorienting. As the cold dark dawn leapt into a pink haze, shades of cobalt and sapphire and dazzling turquoise filled the horizon. Alice picked up her pen, her hand darting across the page as she balanced the notepaper on her lap, her rushed, slanted copper-plate script wonky and uneven.

'Dear Sebastian, it has taken war to make me realize that a life filled with regret is no life at all, and that we owe it to ourselves and those we have lost to make the most of what it brings to us. Love Alice.' She glanced towards the white crests on the rocks, and her former life seemed to melt away. Tucking the note into an envelope, she wondered if, when she posted it, it would ever reach him.

Chapter 3

'Would you like to have a portrait painted?' The question took Edward by surprise, not least because the words – in English, but with a nasal musical accent – felt so sudden, and because the young woman who spoke had materialized apparently out nowhere.

He spun round and saw the beret, pulled down about the ears and that green floral dress.

Aurélie Deschamps extended her hand and Edward, standing before her, still a little bemused, shook it gently. She must have recognized him, since her smile betrayed that she was pleased to see him.

He was transfixed by her face, the kind, wide-open eyes, the small, fine nose that turned upward a little at the end, the elfin profile.

A little shyly, she ventured again: 'A picture. Why not?' Still smiling, she pointed at her sketchbook.

Edward nodded, dumbstruck by the girl's sweet face.

Aurélie carried on, gesturing him to walk beside her.

'How long have you been in Amiens?'

'About a month... I was wounded.'

She glanced at Edward's stick. 'I hope not too badly?' she said, with sadness in her voice.

'No, not badly.'

A silence fell between them which was not awkward. Edward liked it in Amiens. He could eat and drink whenever he pleased. He could wash every day and take off his clothes at night. He had as much sleep as he wanted. He could smell flowers instead of dead bodies and he was not shelled; now there was even a woman. What more could he want?

He gazed at her neck and the little silver cross nestling at the base. 'I should tell you that I am married,' he said.

Aurélie glanced back, her eyes sparkling. She whispered mischievously, 'Well then, in that case, I shall draw your picture and you can send it to your wife.'

They shook hands and arranged to meet again.

That had been on Sunday. Today, at teatime, Edward stood in the crowded street, where the cobbles glistened yellow and mauve, his heart bitter and heavy. What was the point of meeting this girl? Upon reflection, there seemed no purpose in it. It felt as if she were a symptom of all that had gone wrong, an inevitable consequence of the desolation that the war had affected on his impressionable, isolated state.

If he met with this woman now, it would bring disaster. He would make her a victim of his own tragic experience. He would not see her out of revenge for what he saw as the adulterous crimes he believed Alice had committed.

With that thought, he closed his mind and heart against her. He would meet her only out of duty; he did not like to break his word.

It was a traditional troubadour house, with two floors and windows at each level. The shabby painted front door creaked open and Aurélie's pale fingers appeared from behind. She smiled as if she could never know the anguish that had led him to her.

The hallway was clean and plain. Beside the lamps and table there was no other furniture and the room felt empty. Edward's stick echoed on the flagstone floor. Two wooden doors opened on to another room, and that one felt full. Two sofas, an armchair and a packed bookshelf had been squashed in to make room for a piano.

Light streamed in from a door leading into the conservatory. There, among ferns, lay a wooden easel and a pot containing paint brushes.

Aurélie invited her subject to sit down. She wore a pale-blue polka-dotted dress that hugged her at the waist. A loose knot of hair had fallen on to her round shoulders.

It was a burning afternoon and the air hung limpidly under the glass roof, although through the small open window a light breeze flowed gently enough to make the inquisitive sunlight feel less overbearing.

It was hard to know where to begin. Edward sat down awkwardly, still in pain from the wound in his side. Aurélie began to sketch, her eyes darting from time to time in his direction.

'How were you wounded?' she asked, the pencil still scraping against the crisp, white paper pad.

Edward did not want to talk about his wound, or how he had acquired it. 'I don't remember much,' he said. He glanced at his watch and was grateful for the cigarette, rolling the paper into a tube into which he placed the French tobacco, powdered like rosemary.

Aurélie had stopped drawing. Leaning forward a little, she gazed at him. 'When did you marry?' she asked, resuming her work, but still avidly concentrating on Edward.

'Just before the war.'

'And what is she like?'

Edward watched the light streaming through the leaves. In his mind images of the past rose one by one as lucidly as they had ever done and more vividly than any artist's impression. Alice was sitting on the couch at the Coberg's party, exactly as he had first glimpsed her. She was chatting with Evengeline, and a cat was sitting on her lap. In the next instant he saw her sleeping. He could feel the warmth of her breath.

Instantly, he erased the picture from his mind. Where Alice was concerned his heart was constructed of stone, like the hearts of the carved stone martyrs who looked down upon him in the cathedral.

As he came to his senses an elderly lady was standing in the doorway. She was Aurélie's Aunt Marie. Her long white hair fell down the length of her back in a plait and she wore a checked apron. Her face was thin and pale, her skin wrinkled, her black piercing eyes were bloodshot. There was something cloying about her perfume.

'Will you be staying for supper?' said the old woman, nodding her head in the direction of Aurélie. 'My beautiful niece should love it…'

'I have to get back soon, I'm afraid,' replied Edward, bestowing something halfway between a smile and a frown upon his companions.

'You would be welcome to stay,' interjected aunt Marie quickly.

The artist carried on with her work, apparently attempting to conceal her embarrassment with diligence.

At length, after the nose had been drawn and redrawn three times, he made his excuses.

'There,' said the girl at last who, passing him the masterpiece. She was somewhat crimson-faced.

Edward studied the picture with interest. It was a fair likeness. There was a tinge of melancholy in his expression.

'May I buy it?' he asked.

'It's a gift,' said Aurélie. 'For your wife.'

'Then I must find a way to thank you.'

Regarding her thoughtfully, Edward felt the impulse of a strange, unchartered warmth. He kissed her hand as he left, though the glance that she gave made him think that was ill-advised.

A little later, he decided against joining the others in the community room. It was not to avoid the stories that irked and irritated him; there were other old wounds that had reopened and now they bled more bitter regrets. Out of a jumble of memories he could discern clearly an image that awakened echoes within him from his childhood. He was a little boy running outside stone walls behind which his mother was planning his life. He could hear Schubert's Quintet while behind him his friends lay in the mud. Suddenly, he recalled his father's recent letter and the abject disappointment it contained, along with his frustration at how Alice was being treated. Edward had thrown it in the wastepaper basket, but the letter's contents had stayed with him. The words hurt, just as his mother's silence on the matter irked him because in her eyes she had been right all along. No woman was good enough for him.

Pacing the room, fists clenched, evidently so disturbed by his memories that even his fellow patients failed to vex him further, he saw Alice as she had been before he left England, with her soft silvery outline, her sweet head resting on the golden pillow of her loosened curls, the faint enigmatic smile that played about her lips. He heard her play Bach's 'Prelude in C Major'.

What was this love, so tainted and abused, that refused to leave him? If the war were to blame for its ruin, he might be able to look for some higher purpose in everything that had happened. But circumstance alone was not culpable. Something far worse had played its inevitable, hopeless part – and that was character. If he could only live life without the burden of the hopeless memories, maybe he might be able to put everything behind him, but just when he thought he had buried his lost dreams, they came alive again to haunt him.

In this moment, as he imagined Alice and Jasper standing together, an unbearable torrent of blind, jealous rage ripped straight through him. The emotion infuriated him. Even after all this time he had no evidence, but his mother, his life-long ally, had sworn Alice's guilt. Who was he to doubt her word, even if his father as usual said nothing?

Try as he might, he could not stop thinking of how he would avenge himself of what he saw as an unforgivable betrayal. He had been made to look a fool. Love was dead and could never be resurrected. With nerves as twisted as his reasoning, he imagined himself, revolver in his unwavering hand, finger poised at the trigger. He heard mocking, sneering laughter and smelt the stale, rancid brandy on a man's breath. He saw yellow teeth glisten in a red mouth. Then he saw the two lovers entwined together in an embrace. Feeling sick to his stomach and about to burst, he saw Jasper's confused, impertinent smile become a smirk of denial as he protested his innocence, until the terrified grimace of his death finally took its place.

When, at dawn, the order arrived from his Company Commander summoning him to duty, he prepared himself, but the news was not unwelcome.

Chapter 4

Alice began the day in a philosophical mood, carrying out her routine duties without a fuss. She oversaw the new VADs carrying their sputum cups and bedpans, hardly noticing the fetid odour of gangrene. She felt ready for whatever was to be thrown at her, and for that reason alone was glad to be back in Chelsea.

By now she knew a great many things about wounds. She had seen men with missing noses and ears, missing limbs and missing eyes, and she knew how dirt affected the damage. She had seen what dressings could do to and how some injuries healed and others failed. She no longer expected things to go her way, hopeful merely that she could finish her own tiny part in this evil conflict in a way that might prove worthy of those who had suffered and lost their lives.

Every day brought news of fresh tragedy. On her return from Scotland she had heard that Sir Charles Spicer had perished at Langemarck and she had heard from his close friend Bertie Swift that Jasper had been injured at Verdun. There was no information about Hugh Coberg's fate.

The screen was drawn over number nine. Nurse Violet held the corners tightly and Alice changed his bandages, while the lifeless body lay like an old stocking. He was seventeen and his lungs were so bad that every breath was a struggle.

It was easy to fill his shattered shoulders with plugging,

but another matter altogether to remove them. Six inches deep or more and the gauze became stuck, cracking under the pull of forceps, with blood and pus oozing from the cavities. She knew about wounds in the mind and the damage they did in the memory and in the soul. She had seen how shellshock turned even the best of men into blithering wrecks whose legs jerked uncontrollably.

'What is wrong with me?' asked Maurice Jacks, after peering over at his neighbour, only to find the bed was empty. The blood that had come from his lips was in a bowl too high for him to see.

'Shrapnel.' Alice held the jagged, metal fragment that had been buried there these past six months. She studied it, feeling the sharp, spikey edge on one side with her forefinger, the other side smooth and crooked. The number 40 was plainly engraved on it. It smelt bitter. It might just as well have been love itself, sharp and creeping, inflicting wounds that no operation on earth could remove.

'Naarse!' called number eleven. He was a burly, bullish man who could not read or write. He sat up in bed, alert, while his ulcers were being dressed.

Alice looked up.

'I can't keep my mouth closed. Can you 'elp?' He seemed pleased with his quip.

Alice put it down to the alcohol. They had had small bottle of stout to say goodbye to number nine.

She leant at the bedside, deep in concentration. Dressing ulcers was not a straightforward task. It was perfectly possible to unwind a bandage, but the art was not to ask about the origin of the wound. It had become an unspoken act of diplomacy never to mention the subject, since both parties knew the wound would never heal.

The letter to Sebastian remained in her apron pocket

all day. At the end of her shift she posted it in the box outside the hospital.

A fortnight passed before she received any response, and when it arrived the short telegram, unsigned and undated, felt rather disappointing. The message omitted specific details of his arrival and contained no mention of where they should see each other, except that he would be returning to the Great Western Thursday week.

Adamantly she vowed that she would not go to meet him at Victoria Station, which she believed to be jinxed. So where should she wait? Perhaps she would walk with him in the hospital garden. Briefly she wondered about loitering outside the staff cloakroom where they had first chatted, but that idea she also discarded. She carried on as usual with her ward duties, where she did not have to pretend to be occupied, because she genuinely was.

The long-awaited Thursday arrived and the situation in the ward felt impossible. At least five of the patients were dying, and the cries of delirious voices combined with the ravings of two or three coming round from anesthetic turned the ward into chaos. One poor man insisted on lying on the floor and even the slightest noise sent him jumping into the air or hiding under the bed.

At ten past six she stepped outside, where the cries from within the building were muted. There. She pulled the straying lock of hair that had fallen across her face and pinned it back into position. Just for a second she forgot the pandemonium of the morning and the feverish excitement of suspense she had felt earlier. The buildings of the city were silent, lit only by the reflection of the gentle stars that had begun to edge through the gables.

She gathered herself sufficiently to walk over to the wooden bench and sit down, when she glanced up from her watch, there was Sebastian. He looked thin and tired. His cheeks were pale but they flushed as he smiled.

They strolled together beneath the tall plane trees and the sleepy chirping of sparrows. Reaching the river, they spoke of happier times and small, ordinary things that did not betray the unbearable power of their feelings, as if to disguise them from the world and from each other. The ground slipped beneath their feet and the rushing, swirling water seemed to carry them along in its current.

Sebastian walked half-silhouetted, fighting back the words that so unremittingly churned inside him, as if the maimed, hopeless sentences were exploding there.

Unable to endure this intolerable emptiness, Alice moved awkwardly away and, in a soft whisper, said, 'Well, I'm rather tired. I must go home.' She was about to hold out her hand, but he turned with her.

When they reached the Albert Bridge, that same bridge where Edward had stood so long ago when he had first met Alice, Sebastian turned. 'I'm in love with you,' he said, grabbing her by the waist. His face was so close she could feel his breathing.

She surrendered her mouth to his burning kisses, despising herself as she tasted their sinful freedom. When footsteps hurried along the pathway it felt almost a form of deliverance. As the sound petered off into the distance, Sebastian stood watching the water as if he might hurl himself into its depths. But then, from somewhere behind he felt his hand being taken gently.

She shivered as he took her into his arms, as if she had been raided, limp and overcome by the war that raged within her, which seemed greater than any battle.

Chapter 5

In the bars and cafés of the Henriville quartier the beer brimmed and the air was thick with cheap Gauloise cigarette smoke. Loud laughter echoed around the Place de Grambert and the songs of men trying to forget the war resounded at the American bar, which was packed with the Royal Flying Corps, or the Suicide Club, as it was known. In the rue de Jacobin the small quiet back yard was packed with the staff cars of rear-line officers who had parked them there while they ate dinner at Godberts.

Edward and Aurélie were a little late for their booking, but at the desk the smiling, plump *patronne* ushered them through the lobby with its magnificent stained glass ceiling without complaint.

The table was prepared, complete with white linen napkins, a perfectly ironed tablecloth, candles and a tiny vase filled with fresh daisies.

Edward had reached the conclusion that he would have gone mad long ago had it not been for his meetings with Aurélie. He always looked forward to seeing her. He could confide in this charming girl his innermost secrets and she listened to him with such interest, her kind eyes fixed on his. She seemed to hang on his every word, so much so that it felt as if his entire spirit was being healed in the balm of her gaze. She had a dignity that could only have come through suffering and a refinement he found refreshing after the vulgarity of army life.

He had known her for six months and in that time his condition had improved considerably. The wound on his side ached far less; his leg, once raw and torn, no longer required the constant support of his stick. She loved to hear him play the violin she had found, and she would often draw or paint him as he played soulful *chansons*.

He told himself that they were connected by a love of music and a pure, innocent friendship quite different to any other he had experienced. It helped that as they talked they were able to enjoy the best red wine in France and eat the best food.

There were regularly about a hundred and fifty soldiers dining at the Chat Bleu, from every imaginable regiment. Dinner cost forty francs, but money had lost its value. What man with an appetite would not have an expensive dinner if he knew it would be his last?

On this occasion Edward ordered the *truite saumonée avec sauce Americaine* followed by the *glace ephémère*. Aurélie was having the *langouste à la tartare*.

'Are you all right?' asked Aurélie.

'It reminds me of my wife,' he said, glancing at the piano. A smart dark-haired gentleman with a waxed moustache in a bow tie was playing ragtime on the piano.

These days he told Aurélie exactly what he was thinking. He bared every truth to her, even his desire for Alice, the occasional ferocious torrent of his jealousy and his decision to turn his back on what had happened. He explained to her, as if he were talking himself into it, why he had not wanted to write to his wife or to return home, not even for the sake of his parents.

Aurélie nursed his wounded spirit. Sometimes her eyes were faraway, as if she was remembering stories she had heard of English gentlemen and their gallantry, recalling the extraordinary exploits of good people against the Germans. She cajoled Edward, pandered to him; she wrapped him up in the cashmere blanket of her adoration. Aware of the fragile state of his heart, she sat with patience like an artful counsellor. Only when Edward had exhausted his thoughts, however illogical, did Aurélie speak of her own past – the father who had been stolen from her when the Germans had invaded, the mother who visited his grave at the Madeleine cemetery and played sad songs in honour of his memory.

Often Aurélie spoke of her elderly aunt Marie who had never been to school and had never travelled abroad, but who had more brains than an Alsatian. Even now, Marie would not be able to tell you whose side the French were on. Of all the political figures it was Georges Clemenceau, the Prime Minister, that she knew the best. She admired him on account of his enormous bushy moustache, which resembled that of Ghenghis Khan, who she had heard had killed forty million people. But she had read that he had had a difficult upbringing and so forgave him; because of the confusion, her crush had extended to both men.

Aurélie's eyes sparked guiltily as she recounted the tale one evening, pushing the little meringue *isles* around her bowl, but she could see something was awry with Edward, whose own expression betrayed a deeper malaise than his usual melancholy. However hard she tried, it seemed she could not persuade him to manage even the faintest smile.

'What is it?' she asked at last, with a lick of her spoon.

Edward, unable to look at her, took another sip of wine.

'Are you going to England to see Alice?'

'No.' Edward uttered a short, ironic laugh.

A long silence descended which felt strained, while the one or two of the other diners appeared to glance across, as if evesdropping on their conversation.

'You seem different today,' said Aurélie, placing her pale, delicate hand on his arm, as if trying to comfort him.

'I am going back...' As he said it he felt his spine tingle and the muscles of his legs ache.

Aurélie was staring at him in confusion.

'I'm afraid I volunteered,' he said, 'You know how stubborn I am.'

A smile briefly triumphed over Aurélie's gloom and appeared on her lips. At that point the carafe and glasses were brought. Edward poured out some cognac and drank greedily and nervously. He wanted to reap the drinker's share of forgetfulness.

Aurélie's face crumpled with despair and Edward, who in his heart felt already like a dead man, was cast into turmoil. Could he be in love with Aurélie?

For a while they sat and talked, as if only they two were in the room and no one else there existed, their eyes fixed on each other.

Edward played with his half-empty glass. The pianist began an upbeat song and the hubbub around them suddenly felt deafening. Aurélie wanted to leave.

Hand in hand, they began down the cobbled street together towards Aurelie's front door.

'Do you think it is possible to forget the past?' she asked him in a voice that had no edge of bitterness,

Underneath he shuddered. He begged her, 'I think we should never go back. Let it fade, never to return.'

Perhaps inside he did not really mean it, but his tongue had stumbled upon the right thing to say. He clung to what he thought to be the truth, which he had been determined not to relinquish.

'You helped me at a time when I most needed it,' he

said, 'and I shall always be grateful.'

He could feel himself welling up. He pulled her towards him so that she would not see his face. He dared not move in case it might break her.

He wanted to talk to her, but it was as if he was dumb. The words would not come and there was no language on earth to convey what he felt. His hopes had been dashed, along with his dreams.

They fell silent, looking at each other, united by a single thought, knowing instinctively that they understood each other. Somewhere in the middle was a kiss, indistinct, blurred in the guilt and confusion of the moment. His neck tingled with a strand of her hair.

Aurélie closed the front door, holding the scent of him on her collar like a rose he had presented to her. Edward did not look back, but some way off he turned to listen, and in the stillness thought he could hear weeping.

Chapter 6

A Union Jack flew at half-mast over the hospital, black and misshapen against the deepening blood-red sun. The shadow of war seemed to have darkened in the billowy clouds that blended into the purple, silent and never-ending.

Staff Nurse Alice made her way along the corridor. Her starched white apron and cuffs felt stiff and uncomfortable, and the clattering of her patent leather lace ups echoed in her ears. The cape made her feel old, although she was proud of the silver service badge on her right lapel.

Slowing, she paused at the doorway, entranced by the shaft of light streaming through the dispensary window. There was beauty in the weights, globes and jars glinting on the shelf, just as in the whirl of white icicles that hung from the emergency hut outside in the yard, or in the quiet dignity of Geoffrey Hudson, who had slipped away without complaint last night, although he must have been in agony. He had gangrene in both legs.

Hudson was not the only gas case. There had been sixty-three others that week, all with their suppurating blisters and sticky eyes that needed constant dressing. Infections were causing havoc. What use was the extra three shillings in her pocket every week if she was unable to save anyone? She smoothed down her apron. By the time she had reached the top of the stairs she had composed herself.

At 7 a.m. sharp she began a list. Swabs were low and they were almost out of syringes and God knows how many gauzes were needed. Three pints of sodium citrate and sodium hypochorite mix should see them through the week. Halfway down she added twenty-five bottles of morphine and the same again of heroin. After she had finished she emptied bedpans. She had long become accustomed to the drabness of the stultifying routine at the hospital, and the unimaginative discipline. Whatever training, experience or rank a nurse might have had she was not permitted to imagine that this entitled her to any kind of privileges.

Since the declaration of their feelings she had seen Sebastian just three times. Accepting that work took priority, the days that passed before she was able to seek solace in his arms again seemed an eternity. She could hardly wait for the weekends when, out of uniform, she had become accustomed to visiting his house on the electrified Metropolitan line.

On the crowded, sweaty train she found solace outside the window, haunted by the absurd idea of marrying him. Head against the glass pane, the autumn breeze brought back to her the green smells of woodland walks she had once shared with Edward. The air that entered the carriage had a sense of purity, and in the confusion of fresh, heady scents, she remembered the sandalwood that came from Edward's hair. Her eyes fixed on a distant valley, and she could picture him clearly in her memory, his gentle smile, playful and sensitive, that grew at the corners of his mouth, or the way he moved his head. Then she remembered that he was gone.

She had not seen the Cobergs since the summer. Might they know something she did not? The eroding guilt for not contacting them weighed heavily, but whenever she set eyes on Sebastian she felt as if the mortal danger she experienced in London dissipated. It was a strange form of deliverance. The weak, reactive feelings of her schoolgirl heart, of her young marriage and love for Edward, had faded and that brief conjugal life felt like a dream that the war had forced her to wake from. The idea that this new love might too come to an end tortured her even more intensely. If she was to lose Sebastian as well, she would never recover.

Armed with a small overnight bag containing her lavender *eau de toilette*, a filmy *négligé* and a pair of mule satin slippers, as she pressed the doorbell her heart thudded.

She was just about to turn her back and walk away when the door swung open and any apprehension and regret she had felt disintegrated. Sebastian covered her cheeks with kisses.

Later, behind closed doors, after she had given herself to him wholly and completely, she sat on his lap, her naked toes brushing the crumpled pile of stockings on the pale carpet, as she played with his hair between her pink fingers.

They spoke about the blackberries growing among the hawthorn bushes, about the chickens in the yard and their fresh eggs, about the cygnet ring that Sebastian wore on his third right-hand finger, but not about the hospital, the raids, or about music and in particular not about Edward and her own missing ring.

'How long do we have?' Immediately she knew it had been a mistake to ask.

'I leave tomorrow,' sighed Peterson.

She flung her arms around his neck as if upon his mercy. Pressing her flushing cheek against his, she could hardly ask the name of the destination. He offered it anyway: he was going to that place, the same one that had silenced her first love. He might just as well have called it death.

'For how long?' A torrent of fear flooded through her

bones and her throat felt constricted.

'I'm not sure.'

What if this were simply an excuse? Hastily scrutinizing Peterson's expression, she was forced to abandon her suspicion; his eyes revealed such despair that no scheme could have lain hidden behind them.

An agonizing, leaden silence fell. Sebastian swallowed, as if something had closed his throat.

'Must you go?' whispered Alice.

The response was a kiss. 'I'll write every day, I promise.'

'It is not the first time I have heard those words...'

Peterson, sensing the shadow of the absent rival of whom they had never spoken, began to bristle. However indirect the referral, given everything that had happened, he felt forced to rise and walk to the window. The air in the room had become overbearing. He had never met Edward or even seen him. He may have gone, but from what he knew it was certainly possible that Alice still loved him.

The bubble of his jealousy lingered oppressively for a few seconds until she came to him. The feather kisses, placed with precision across his forehead, soothed his troubled nerves.

Alice stepped down from tiptoe and laid her head against his chest, as if finding a refuge there. The peace lasted no more than an hour before the motor cab came to take her to the train station. She felt his soft, deep breath on her ear and dared not move a fingernail as the agony of pulling away from him drew near.

Much later, wrapped up in her mohair scarf, she put pen to paper, and the jumbled fragments of a young woman's longing tumbled onto the page. The passion was not for any man, but rather an unfulfilled aching of a soul that felt destined to be alone.

Chapter 7

Edward waited on the platform. He felt much better. He was freshly shaved and washed. His uniform had been laundered but starched shirt still emitted a stale, sour smell. At least the shrapnel under his rib cage no longer burned and cramped whenever he moved, although he could feel it when he breathed.

The Gare d'Amiens was packed. The thick tide of the crowd surged around him and a strange murmur issued from its midst. In the sea of khaki a freckled face brightened and the expression of utter disbelief became a broad, familiar grin.

'Edward!'

A breathless and excited Harry Lloyd, who had been waiting for hours on the other side of the rails, gripped hold of his old friend's arm. Their eyes met.

'Good lord!' exclaimed Edward in astonishment.

It had been almost three years since they had set eyes on each other. Before either could say anything else the locomotive clanked and puffed into the station and the two Tommies heaved their kit bags over their shoulders, squeezed their way on to the carriage and sat down opposite each other.

Harry, still reeling from surprise, lit up a Gauloise. He was on his way to Bosinghe. 'So where the devil have you been?'

Stumped as to where to begin, Edward reached for the right words and sentences to explain his long silence. 'I've been a bit tied up,' he said at last. 'How is everyone?'

By 'everyone' he meant Alice, and Harry was under no illusion of that fact. 'Your wife is well,' said Harry.

'And you?' asked Edward.

'Surviving.'

Edward grinned. Survival was no mean achievement in the present circumstances.

The two men looked hard at each other's faces, each registering the gaunt, thin sallowness in the cheeks of the other, and the little wisps of white in the hairs around their ears. The subtle changes seemed so similar in appearance that they might have been regarding a mirror.

'Do you still play?' asked Harry.

'I have a new weapon,' said Edward, clutching his rifle.

Harry laughed. A thoughtful look came across his face. 'No rehearsals for us this time...'

Half an hour later, as the train drew into St Elioi the two old friends wished each other luck. As Harry climbed off Edward wondered if he would ever see him again.

Seeing Lloyd had brought everything back. The mention of Alice irked and needled at him. Without another thought, he banished her, and as the swirls of steam outside the window evaporated, her image was replaced by Aurélie, with her searching, fearful, beautiful eyes and dark sleek hair, just as he had left her the previous evening.

He reported for duty at battalion headquarters, a ramshackle group of derelict-looking stone buildings they called Crest Farm. It was about a mile away from Rozestraat, and the shellfire was deafening.

There was a feeling of bitterness among the men at the barracks. They had been through a very rough fight at Ypres and in the charge with the Royal Scots two hundred and fifty men had been either wounded, killed or gone missing.

The gas used by the Germans seemed stronger than before and this had induced hatred. It turned the face blue. It closed the throat and shut down the body in slow, agonizing bursts. Repulsed by such inhumane methods of warfare, the men concluded the Germans were capable of any evil possible.

Less than an hour later the brigadier, accompanied by his two subordinate officers, brought in the mail. Usually the drama of suspense that descended upon the men as letters and telegrams were distributed in the officer's mess was so tense it caused the ruddiest of faces to turn ashen. Edward was uneasy. A few odd letters had been forwarded to him in Amiens, mainly from his family, but the majority, sent care of his regiment, had lain waiting for him at battalion HQ.

Each man received his envelopes and walked without speaking across the bare, straw-strewn barn floor, disappearing from sight one after the other, behind one of the bales of hay or further beyond the yard, so that any uncontained emotion might be released in private.

The brigadier had to call out the name twice before Edward responded. He took the neat, fat bundle bound tightly with jute string. The blood ebbed from his face and his throat dried. He nodded his thanks and then his shadow slipped quietly away – and with it the man.

Behind the shed, at a safe distance from the others, he found a mound of sandbags and settled himself there, surrounded by spades, picks, barbed wire, spare duck walks and other trench paraphernalia.

His fingers sifted anxiously through the pile. He recognized Alice's slanting hand on the first few envelopes. The rest were from his mother, apart from a few postcards from friends.

He decided to open the telegram first. It was dated 7th July 1916, fourteen months ago.

'Grandfather died. Come back soon. Your Alice.'

He read the words again, thinking that perhaps he might have misunderstood them the first time around. He read them yet again, but there was no denying their meaning.

The words began to smudge. A raindrop had smeared the page. Surrounded by the muffled, indistinct strands of his past, he decided to open the other letters later, after the dried eggs and sardines had been turned into something tasteless that was supper.

When he returned to the exact same place and the precise sandbag, he had lost track of time completely. He knew it was late because it was dark, save for the solitary gas lamp that lit the sheen of drizzle. Occasional flashes of light illuminated the sheets of paper as he removed his helmet, but he barely noticed the confused blur of noise still echoing in the blackness.

His mother wrote of insignificant matters. She told him that she was well and looked forward to his return, but that last letter was dated almost a year earlier and it made no mention of Alice.

Teeth chattering, he read Alice's later account of her grandfather's long illness with astonishment. In this long letter, dated October 1915, she implored him to write to her. She did not appear to have received his own letters, including the one he had posted in the mailbox on the route from Sedan.

Still reeling from the news of William's death, one by one he opened her other letters, but as the dates were muddled and he could make no sense of them. He was surprised to discover the revelation in the second letter he opened, which was dated even earlier in 1915, containing the news that she had become a nurse. But the real bombshell came in a later note. It told how Jasper Lenz had been almost thrown out of the army as a result of a close friendship with another soldier.

The flimsy paper slipped from his fingers. He picked up the muddied, wafer-thin sheet and the ink ran in wet, vertical lines. Sitting there alone, under the darkening sky, his body felt damp, his soul was saturated in regret, rushing through his veins, ravaging and consuming him. He realized his former suspicions had been completely unfounded.

'My darling, what has happened to you? The months pass by and still no news of you. The suspense suffocates me. I implore you. If you are alive, let me know? I shall love you forever, hold you in my heart for eternity...'

A lump rose in his throat and his eyes welled with tears. No matter how hard he tried to hold them back, they streamed down his face in rivers. 'How could she possibly have written to me in this way?' he wondered in amazement. Surely, if nothing else, her words proved that she did love him. He drew out the locket from his breast pocket and held it in his palm, torn, conflicted. It was impossible to know what to believe.

Later, he lay stretched on his bunk, head propped on one elbow, searching for a clue to any infidelity in her words, reading them over and over again, until finally in exhaustion his head dropped among the papers.

It was her fifth letter, dated just a few months earlier, which made sleep impossible. It consisted of only a few lines, but read as a cry of despair. The unfinished business felt unbearable. It seemed unlikely they might be able to rescue the marriage after so long. The trust between them had been eroded. They would always be searching to find if they remained true to each other. Each of them might never tell and eventually they would hate each other. Despite all these things he had to talk it through with her. Then he remembered he could not leave. Desertion was punishable by death.

The next morning his platoon leader, a stout beer-bellied man named Forrester arrived bearing news. Cheerily, and with a firm handshake, he informed Edward he had been billeted to the Transport Section of No 2 Company a few miles off from the road at Messines. He gave Edward a chit summoning him to a team briefing.

His new job was running field ambulances, keeping a detailed account of events and sending them in the requisite green envelope direct to the Colonel. It was a soft job, and he didn't care about the promotion. He didn't want to be a hero any more. Courage, he had concluded, was not about duty, but the thin, frail thread of allegiance to a country and the ongoing sense of brotherhood that gave a man the strength to carry on.

That afternoon, together with a small party, Edward stood in the driving, freezing rain before what was left of the Cloth Hall. The roof had gone entirely and the belfry was badly damaged. Not a mile away, St Martin's Cathedral was barely recognizable, the Cloister Gate reduced to rubble. Even the cobbles of the streets had been obliterated.

Ypres was known as the city of fear and, glancing around at the torn, cracked buildings, an atmosphere of foreboding and malevolence permeated every crevice. It was filled with ghosts, echoes and shadows, but as Edward glanced around at the battered ruins, he was not thinking about the hundreds of thousands of living and dead who passed through but of the broken, dissolute carnage of his marriage. For the first time since the war had begun he was feeling that he had misjudged Alice. Perhaps it was he who had been unfaithful.

Ahead, a confusion of forsaken trenches, churned up and scorched, remained off-bounds because so many unexploded shells still lurked there. Twenty yards off those, where the stretchers were being brought in, was the base from which Edward would be receiving and transporting the wounded. Most men asked only for water or a cigarette; those with stomach wounds groaned.

The platoon commander explained with gesticulating arms and without once pausing between sentences that the injured needed to be brought back here from the Advanced Aid post, which was situated in a mineshaft near the village of Wieltje, not far from Langemarck. A shallow stream required the constant use of pumps to prevent flooding, but at least it was safe from shellfire.

Stretcher-bearers carried the wounded from Aid Posts to the mineshaft, where they were redressed and carried a mile to St Jean Corner. From there the injured were transferred in ambulances and conveyed to Crest Farm, and from there, on to the Casualty Clearing Station.

Edward watched the lights in the sky, recognizing the sounds each produced – the flamethrower's boom that could burn a man alive; the trench mortar that could send dozens flying into the air with its terrifying thundering; the shells that made a great 'crump' noise, followed by a sound like crockery falling from a tray as roof tiles shattered on the ground. The coal boxes, as they were known, were black and came with terrifying explosions. Interspersed with the guns and shells, he could hear men's voices carried on the wind.

From where he was standing, he could see black became purple-blue. The blood-orange sun had long been blotted out by rain. In the atrocious weather conditions the ground had become a quagmire. Shell holes had filled with slime and tanks had become stuck in the mud. Six men were needed per stretcher and the enemy shelled the stretcher-bearers mercilessly. Chits arrived regularly containing impossible orders. Edward replied that the instructions were noted, without any intention of carrying them out.

What madness urged him to venture out to that mineshaft one evening remained unknown. Several men he had fought with in the Fourteenth at Zillibeke were now attached to B Company. Harris, who had also been promoted, had his party of twenty-five men waiting in the darkness. They were on their way from brigade HQ and were carrying medical kits. Without a guide it was not an easy journey back to the deep dugouts. Time and time again they had climbed over waterlogged disused trenches that had once formed the second line, tripping over wire and tearing their clothes. The mud was deep, the men were tired and their legs and feet became stuck.

Edward led the way as an explorer might have approached an expedition to the Pole. His feet were already numb and cold and he could hardly feel his fingers, but something was going wrong at St Jean Corner. The 109th Field Ambulance had been shelled.

Harris brought up the rear. They moved in single file along the sunken road, a river of mud in places two feet deep. On the right signallers, orderlies and runners huddled together to stay warm. On the left other men crouched, using the bank for cover. It was impossible to see how the runners got to and from Batallion HQ in this weather.

Wading past the empty trenches, Edward halted. Something lay in the way. It was a man.

'What are you doing?' asked Edward.

'Sorry, sir, I'm finished,' mumbled the man. He clutched at his medical bag.

'Come on! Get up! Don't you think all these men are done?'

'Sorry, sir.'

'What's going on?' called an agitated Harris from the back.

Edward wiped more mud on to his brow with his right hand, though he had intended to wipe it off. 'You know if you don't get up it's my duty to shoot?'

'Yes, sir, if you must.'

Cursing, Edward picked up the medical kit and moved on, slipping and sliding, avoiding the shell holes and the bodies that had been thrown there. He heard Harris shouting. A shot rang out, but he didn't look back.

The trench at the Corner had become a great gully, the bottom of which was so deep in mud it was necessary to keep to the sides. Someone had placed a blanket over the men lying at the entrance, but it could not disguise the stench of decaying flesh. Men cowered under their groundsheets at their places below the parapet. How many of those rifles would fire? How were they ever going to get them clean?

In these conditions moving fifty yards could take about half an hour. It quickly became clear that some of the men were stuck at the bottom of the trench could move no further. Shovels were pointless. There were portions that remained impassable unless aided.

Further down, the tunnel had become a cesspool and the pump had stopped working. Mud flowed everywhere, mixed with the filth from the overfull latrines and decomposing bodies. Edward waded waist-deep into the river of mud and his hands, pink lilies, skimmed the surface. Muck clung to the rifle, and the bayonet cut through, a hot knife. He could not feel his legs.

He gulped and gulped, swallowing the mud that seeped from the nape of his neck into his eyes as if his brain had been enveloped. From his gullet it flooded, right down to the soles of his feet. The brown he swam through was the same as the river inside him. Only the thin parchment of his skin kept it separate.

Ahead of him a man floated face-up in the mire. Edward's questioning eyes met his faraway gaze, but it was no use. The empty stare continued and Edward's sudden appearance did nothing to stir him. How many more lost souls were down there? Just as he was asking himself this the ground moved and the air filled with fire. He surfaced into the gloopy air as earth's newborn, caked in its afterbirth. Around him other bodies flew up, their heavy outlines smothering the stars. Blood splashed like tar across arm and black icicles of flesh.

He could hear nothing through his peat-clogged ears, even as he struggled out of the tunnel. Behind him was only smoke. His head was giddy with Alice. He wanted to go to her, to touch her hair, but there were only bodies, men with faces that were no longer their own, their limbs twisted with falling.

The black earth was ugly and infinite, made of jutting limbs and sticky hair, sinewy bones and draping skin. Two shadows moved close together in a mound, resembling a brown pyramid in the faint light green He recognized both soldiers, and lifted the one who was still breathing. Sodden and covered in sludge, somehow he carried Harris. The smell of cordite, mud and sweat mingled in his nostrils. Lice swam over the heavy, wet uniform, the wool gorged with putrid water and mud.

He had accepted this hell, of sodden trenches, crump holes, barbed wire, machine guns, bombs and shelling. He had reconciled the horrors that greeted him here – the crippling disappointment of marriage and the foreboding of warfare. All these things represented the destruction of his innocence and had made him see the world differently. It was simply like refocusing the lenses of his field glasses.

Harris lay in the mire where Edward had placed him. His legs were missing, but he did not complain. The roar of gunfire made the river tremble and shudder and the din made any sense of peace impossible.

'Can I do anything for you, Bob?'

'Straighten my legs.'

Edward touched the bones with his fingertips and that seemed to soothe him.

'Get my wife's photograph out of my pocket.'

Edward took it and put it in the Harris's hands. He could not move, he could not lift a hand or a finger, but somehow he managed to cling to his wife's photograph. There was something in this tight, desperate holding on that made Edward wince, a shard of jealousy he would not admit to and which was out of place.

When the chest slowed and stopped rising, with the utmost tenderness, Edward closed Harris's surprised eyes. No one noticed the water streaming down his cheeks, or the tears that mingled with it. No one saw him bury his red, swollen face into his forearm and curl in the mud like a fetus.

Chapter 8

The first part of the train journey felt too cramped to be anything other than tolerable, but after three long hours Alice's face brightened at the sight of the small stone cottage and the thought of seeing old friends. It seemed almost impossible that such a sanctuary could exist when at night in the city bombers dropped their roaring cargoes, wreaking havoc like manmade vampires over the skies.

She approached via a narrow passage, went through a white wooden gate and approached a green-painted front door surrounded by honeysuckle. Dog roses, peonies and foxgloves decorated the pretty front garden and the scent of sweet briar hung like cologne on the autumn air.

The front door opened and Professor Coberg's milky, translucent eyes twinkled cheerily. 'My dear Alice!'

She could not help throwing her arms around his shoulders. It was wonderful to see him again. He was much changed, stooping heavily, his nostrils bearded and dark hair whitened. He told her about his arthritis, but said nothing of the severe thigh wound he had received when he had been mugged and robbed at the Savoy Theatre on account of his nationality.

Just behind the door she found Helga waiting to welcome her and smother her cheeks with kisses, her heart fluttering with affection. Helga's warmth belied her own developing frailty. Leaning on her walking stick, her genial face reddened with emotion as she communicated to Alice how much she had missed her. 'How are you, my darling girl? Poor thing. You look very pale. No wonder. We must make it better. Oh dear! This awful war!'

They sat in the drawing room and chatted in an atmosphere of delight, doubled by the years of separation and unrest preceeding it. The joy of the reunion notwithstanding, Helga did not forget to ask after Alice's health and that of Rose. With heavy hearts they also discussed Grandfather, and each noted that it was for the best that whatever suffering which had, without doubt, imposed a terrible burden on him, had gone. He was at peace.

The sun was shining in at the two windows and through the glittering drops of rain it cast a broad shaft of light onto the piano. A lump came to Alice's throat.

Her meagre nurse's income barely covered her living expenses and Rose's small salary. From Peterson she would not accept a penny. As the Professor asked her how she was keeping, she wondered how she would be able to eat.

The elderly couple knew that Alice was unhappy and when they heard she had been forced to sell her beautiful harp they treated her even more kindly. Alice was to have the best room and be tempted to eat with every delicacy their local farm had to offer. They did their best, even though Ivy had gone home to Scarborough. Ivy's efforts were concentrated on a small business of her own offering laundry and nowadays when she stayed with the Cobergs she came as a guest rather than a servant.

Lunch was a feast of bacon and potted cheese. They ate at the table in the garden, where the benign sycamores bent their boughs over them and the light filtering through the leaves made a patchwork pattern on the flowers.

After they had finished the stewed apple, with a look of real concern the Professor said, 'You know, you must not let the war defeat you.' He deliberately omitted mentioning Edward's name. He was not sure how much Alice knew and, in any case, Edward's mother had advised him it would be best to say nothing. Edward wanted it that way.

'How funny. Edward once said that to me,' said Alice.

The Professor seemed suddenly unnerved. He crossed his legs and uncrossed them. After all, it had all happened so long ago.

Helga, who had also long been privy to the news from George and Marigold that their son was alive and well, looked as if she was about to cough. 'Edward is not the only young man in the world worth having, and with your pretty face you will never want admirers. The Simpsons and the Martins are coming tonight, which will amuse you. I might even sing.'

'Actually, I feel very fortunate,' sighed Alice.

Weak with fatigue and worn down by the constant air raids and the sudden, fierce violence of the attacks, Alice felt overpowered by regrets, but pride prevented her from divulging her weakness, and shame prevented her telling about Sebastian.

Helga had to take a glass of her favourite herbal tonic before she could be persuaded to tell Alice the fully story of their dear friend Jasper's fate. Promoted to Major, he had been killed leading his men forward in Abbeville.

Alice put down her spoon. She could say no more. She buried her face in her napkin to stifle the tears.

The Professor's sprightly demeanour became mournful as he imparted the details, equally sorrowfully, of Sir Charles Spicer's death at Ploegsteert. Helga's expression became drawn and strained. 'And Hugh?'

'He is alive!' cried Helga. Suddenly there was not a dry eye among the hollyhocks.

Alice remained at the cottage for several days. She was earnestly pressed by Helga to stay longer, but she resolved to be gone by the weekend. Before she left the Professor handed her a slip of paper on which was written an address of a war clinic in south-east London, but other than what could be gleaned from his grim expression imparted very little information about Hugh's injuries.

On Saturday she wasted no time in catching the train from Charing Cross to Denmark Hill with the intention of visiting him.

The Maudsley Military hospital, a red, gabled building covered in creepers rose ahead. It was a gloomy, towering edifice, which stood out against run-down tenement blocks. Golden leaves lay scattered around its imposing stone doorway. Alice had heard about the patients who came here who suffered from psychological traumas, from neurasthenia and functional paralyses to hysteria, notwith-standing the bad cases of shellshock who were locked up.

She walked quickly up the steps, almost tripping with anticipation and nearly forgetting to mention who she was visiting when a shrill voice called after her. 'Can I help you, miss? Do you have an appointment?'

'I am visiting a friend,' said Alice. 'Do you have anyone here named Coberg?'

The staff nurse seemed happy enough to let her go on. She confided with pride that they had a gymnasium, a carpenter's workshop, a garden and even a vegetable patch.

Alice's low-heeled shoes clicked on the stone stairwell and as she hurried along the polished corridor. Her pale blue hat shaded her face and it was not possible to see her eyes, or the strands of hair drawn from her temples by the hot air. She remained incognito.

The ward was a large, high-ceilinged room with bare,

pastel walls. Only a few men lay in their beds. Some were sitting up and playing cards in their grey flannelette dressing gowns. A tall man with a white moustache mumbled incoherently and another, thin, with staring eyes, groaned repetitively.

She walked on purposefully among the patients without really seeing them or having a sense of the man she was looking for although, on every side, all the men saw her. Her delicately arched brows rose as she smiled at the cluster of expectant faces.

Cocooned in her ignorance – for Alice still had no idea about the injustice Hugh had inflicted upon her so long ago with Edward or the damage that caused – the thought of seeing Hugh again after so long filled her with joy, so much so that when she finally spotted the young sergeant her heart soared. In almost the same split second another feeling replaced her excitement, although she was too shocked to register it. It was neither happiness nor fear, but lay somewhere in between.

She recognized him immediately. He was slumped in a chair near the window. His hands rested limply on his lap; his head was slightly tilted. He was staring at the pale lilac wall that seemed to have a soothing effect on him.

She did not expect him to react and for a few moments he failed to see her standing there so near to him.

The first thing she noticed was his head, which had suffered a major catastrophe. The skull had been smashed on one side and, although the opening was healing, the bare flesh was exposed. A papery layer of skin had been carefully grafted over the wound, although it was severe and could not be disguised. By some unknown mercy, his features were still intact.

There were moments when her ability to think or say

anything meaningful failed her and this was one of them. She approached slowly, gently kissed his head and knelt down in front of him.

Hugh looked at her in astonishment, as if he had not received the note she had sent to let him know that she was coming.

'I'm sorry I'm late. You know how useless I am at time-keeping.'

His darted rapidly, as if she was a figment of his imagination.

'How did you find me?' He stuttered, as if to utter the words was an immense achievement.

She began to explain and his shoulders relaxed. "I'm all right,' he said, though clearly he wasn't.

'Would you like to go for a walk?'

He nodded mechanically.

They sat, side by side on the stone bench, watching the play of clouds above the city, allowing the memories of their youth to unfurl mechanically.

Hugh's fingers quivered violently as he knocked the ash from his cigarette. The damaged part of his face was on the other side, as if he wished to spare her the ugly truth of those things from which he felt she should be protected, those secret, terrible truths that only those who had borne witness could know.

She did not look at him too closely, out of compassion rather than a sense of disgust. She tried to picture him as he was before, playing tennis and at her wedding. She remembered his starched collars and his cream linen suit and how he had once gazed at her at a concert where Edward had been playing the violin.

'You haven't changed at all in three years. In fact you are even more beautiful.' He looked back at her from the prison of his disfigurement. 'It doesn't hurt much, you know…'

She squeezed his hand and a feeling of helplessness overwhelmed her. His wound had altered his speech, and what else had the war affected that she could not see?

Hugh sat smoking, from time to time remarking on small, irrelevant things, which might have fooled them both into believing momentarily that all was well with the world and that in different ways their existence had not been shattered by the war after all, as if time had not eroded them. He said nothing of the panic attacks, the night sweats and the dreams from which he woke screaming. Instead he said he had learned to like Beethoven, made light of the fact even that it had taken a shell to make it happen.

Alice knew the truth. She had seen it every day in her own hospital.

'Do you know what happened to Edward?'

Hugh shook his head. He was unable to bring himself to speak of the time he had seen Edward in 1916.

'Do you still play?' He glanced at her once slender hands, the elegant harpist's fingers now chapped and worn.

'I sold my harp.' She had not played for so long, she imagined that she had forgotten how.

Shifting again, he wavered. 'And are you happy?'

'I think so,' she said lightly. 'I met someone.'

He exhaled the smoke from his mouth and allowed it to linger. He felt overcome with emotion. He shifted from side to side a little as if the burden he was bearing had become too heavy, although it could never weigh as much as the burden of his love for her.

'Look, Alice,' he said. He paused. 'You won't be annoyed if I tell you something, will you?'

'Of course not.'

'Well, the fact is…'

He was going to say it, really he was. It was at the tip of his tongue. He was going to confess everything – how he had loved her all those years and how he had gone about deliberately setting Edward against her. He had been ready for whatever consequences his lie brought, but now Alice, his beautiful, perfect first love had given her heart to another. It was all so confused. His head hurt.

At that moment his courage deserted him and he made something up something ridiculous. He glanced at her again, and seeing that she did not suspect anything in his story, relaxed his shoulders.

'I don't suppose you would have dinner with me, would you?' he said.

The irony was that Alice, who remained oblivious to the trouble he had caused in her life, was thinking only of how she might help him overcome his difficulties. She knew that he was asking her not just for dinner, but for more than that. Once she would never have dreamed of giving it to him, but now her fiery, artistic nature, inherited from her father's side, accepted things that she would never have done previously..

Silence fell between them and their secrets remained unspoken. Only the flap of a moth's wings could be heard flickering against the shadows.

Chapter 9

On 16th November 1917, a wet, bitter day, Edward packed up and set off for England for ten days' leave, recalling relatively little those last hours of service, only clambering from the foul communication trench at twice the speed he had achieved when arriving, and that he had lost his mess tin and helmet. Once in the road he had slipped along with the others without complaint, however much those in front were out of line. With every step they had drawn nearer the invisible line the marked the danger zone, closer and closer to the casualty clearing station and on past the familiar old billets.

With long strides he had marched across Hellfire Ridge until the shadow of death was behind him and his heart gone out to the poor devils left behind. With the sprinkling of snow and a sharp frost you might have been forgiven for missing the large craters. Everything looked crisp and white. The cold was bitter, but the freezing mud had spread trench foot like topsy.

He emerged in the spirit of reflection, as if he had earned the right to leave the battlefields. He had given death the chance, but it had not taken it. He had been the victor. How many times did a man have to pawn his soul? Hadn't he earned the right of respite? Would not even the woman who had betrayed him and everything they had stood for together forgive him for this exit, rather than keep offering death his life until it accepted?

For the first time it felt as if he understood what hope meant. It was the constriction of optimism that depressed men in the trenches. 'If' stood before every prospect, every move, and it was no small 'If'. Now the cloying strain of uncertainty was behind him at last. He knew he was not yet free. But he had survived.

Inside he was still bleeding. An inexplicable force had overcome him, something that compelled him that he could not place. It emanated from the heart rather than from the head and had no foundation in reason.

Beyond the promenade dismal grey waves tumbled angrily over one another on the blustery shoreline. He fixed his eyes on the pregnant clouds, and reflected upon what words he could possibly offer Alice. This woman whom he still loved and who was still his wife, was now a stranger. How different she was to Aurélie, the patient, adoring artist in Amiens, with her bright, eager eyes and skin like gossamer. He had heard from Aurélie twice since he had been at Ypres. She had left Amiens and was living in a house built by her father in the countryside.

La Maison d'Henri consisted of several brick farm buildings built in the traditional style with a tiled roof and gabled windows set around a courtyard with a porch gateway. It had an orchard and a few acres of arable land that could be worked to make a living. Situated on the slope of a hill near the Belgian border, at least thirty miles north from the battle lines, it was also safer.

He thought of her with her box of pastels, drawing the countryside. How different life might have been had he given his weary life to her. Aurélie would be content and her aunt would live with them. A cart would carry her paintings to market and he would resume music. In the summertime a kitchen garden would be filled with carrots.

Perhaps they might even have had children.

Since he was too late to catch the afternoon boat, he had to spend the night in Dieppe, where he scarcely slept for the sharp, clawing dread he felt over whether confronting Alice after all this time was the right decision.

Choked and clogged with uniforms, the town seemed to have lost its character in the exigencies of war. It was easier to take refuge behind the thin walls of the hotel, to hide from the icy sea wind that rushed, screaming across the expanse of nothing. He washed and shaved. He was grateful for the thin bed with the mattress that dipped in the middle. Hallucinating dreams haunted his sleep – Fitzroy lying dead on the ground, bodies on barbed wire strung like scarecrows, William Purefoy's kindly smile reflected in the paperweight on his desk. Try as he might he could not paint the face of Aurélie in his tormented mind.

Morning brought no brighter thoughts, and Edward began the rough and prolonged crossing sweaty and fog-headed. He was repelled by the swell of the stormy brown waters. They reminded him of a divide in his life he could not grasp. Whether it was between the past and the present, England and France, or before the war and after it was immaterial. The heavy sky hung over the water, dipping into the depths and reflecting the murkiness of existence, a place of monotone without inspiration.

When had left England cheers had rung out from the pier and blue figures had waved their flags, but now, as they silently drifted in like cargo, and lay waiting, no one noticed. No longer the same sensitive, naïve musician who had once stepped aboard the Calais-bound ship, with his pristine kit and cheery, patriotic gait, the lean, gaunt figure that walked back on to his homeland was changed beyond recognition. He knew how to execute God's justice. He knew how to kill a man.

Squashed up against the rattling door of the carriage, he watched the emerald splashes that flitted past the window, but he felt disconnected from the familiarity that they offered him. He wanted to go back, to abandon this country he remembered so dimly. He wanted to return to Aurélie.

The muddled recollection of his departure three years ago still haunted him. He felt the prickliness of the wool uniforms, smelt the smoke lingering about the men he had travelled with, and heard the loud, raucous singing. In his memory he saw a sea of khaki, until the green splashes turned brown and beige spots mingled with the black smudges. All these impressions were just transitory, fragments of a fugitive jigsaw whose pieces would always be missing.

An air of excitement had come over the troops waiting to reach home. Men with faces older than their years lit up at the thought of being reunited with their families. They had witnessed horror and hardships in the trenches such as they had never imagined possible. They no longer wondered about if or when the war would end, for they had become incapable of imagining life without it.

Victoria Station was dimly lit, especially beyond the barrier where the black trains waited like sleeping snakes. On the platforms khaki figures stood interspersed with civilians, mainly women dressed in dark clothes. Some figures were listless, but those decorated with ribbons, or red and blue tabs looked animated with the adrenaline of self-importance. The lugubrious atmosphere so often pervading the concourse was lightning-charged, the air vibrating with suppressed emotion felt all the more acutely because there was no release for it. The hopes and fears of each and every person standing were shared.

Kit bag in hand, Edward moved awkwardly through the throng, with his rifle, belt and badges. Partly he ached because there was no one to greet him. Partly he brimmed with excitement and hope that it was not too late to salvage his marriage. His mind was a cloud brooding above his body, brimming with violence and revolt so that constant effort was required to keep it in check.

At the flower stall he bought a bunch of Parma violets and his mind jumped an ocean. They reminded him not of Alice, but of his parting with Aurélie.

In the Regent Café he drank coffee in the hope that it would clear the fog of exhaustion misting his judgment. After settling the bill he walked, consumed by his thoughts of Alice, his boots echoing on the hollow pavement. Still wondering if he should telephone, but sensing that might be a mistake, he decided against it. He wanted to shock her. He wanted to turn her universe upside down as Hugh's revelation had done to him.

He began to wonder if he should turn back. What good could really come of this?

On the southern side of the river the industrial quarter remained hardly changed. Barges chugged the length of the river. Nearby the sound of the turbid backwaters, swollen by the recent tides, rushed past and every other sound was lost in the splashing and eddying against the slimy piles on the riverbank.

The setting sun, a furious globe of brass peeking through the black buildings, reminded him of the melting sky that he had seen over the fields of Flanders, there where blood, sun and moon coagulated. Between the black trees Carlisle Mansions remained intact, just as it always had been.

With a shudder of trepidation, he raised his eyes and sought the second floor. He thought he could make out shadows. Three weeks earlier he had kissed Aurélie, pressing her hand against the hallway. He could still smell her musky scent. Beating the air with his cap, he banished the thought of her like a cloud of insects. Try as he might, he could not dispel the bitterness that stuck in his gullet.

He remained standing in the street for a long time, glancing up at the window and down at the front door again, unable to decide whether to go up, and even more fearful about what would happen if he did. He teetered on the precipice of something unspeakable.

People went in and came out. A neat lady dressed in a blue marocain and velvet picture hat with a green glycerine feather opened the door and walked straight passed him without stopping. He did not recognize Kitty Smith.

Crossing to the other side of the street, he raised his eyes once again to the second-floor windows, but only the furthest emanated a faint glow. At that instant the shadows merged. Two figures stood against the window entwined in silhouette.

No one saw him as, dejected and alone, he made his way slowly back towards the Embankment, or the wilted violets that dropped from his shaking fingers into the black water. Hauling his kit, he stumbled slowly along the deserted pathway and plunged once more into the insatiable silence of annihilation. In the reflection of the river he made out the shape of a cross. It marked the burial site of his ravaged heart.

Chapter 10

Alice had no regrets over what had happened with Hugh, and it was she who had been the instigator, softly brushing his neck with her hands and drawing him to her, giving herself to him, as if she were making an offering at a temple. She had done it out of compassion, just as so many other women gave their bodies, as if their flesh was a sacrifice. It was a service they performed, a duty that was required of them. That was all.

Still, when the following morning she discovered the telegram lying on the doormat, she could not help the tinge of shame and guilt that overcame her and the leaden feeling in her heart. The message summoning her was unsigned, and the feeling of circumspect secrecy leant it a special significance. Reading it through, there was no question in her mind that it was from Sebastian. It did not occur to her that it might have been from Edward.

At eleven o'clock she bought an ounce of pear drops at Euston station and took the electrified Metropolitan line to Buckinghamshire, her young heart dancing with happiness and an excitement matched only by her pride. It was as if she had been given a second chance and the man she loved had come back to her after all.

She knew his house well and where it was located. She had visited often over the past couple of months and had her own key. Having knocked, without waiting, she turned it in the lock and burst into the hallway.

'Thank God you're safe,' she gasped as he appeared before her.

Unable to speak with emotion, Peterson buried his head in the dip at the base of her slim neck, slightly moist from her joy, soft and velvety. After the first sweet kiss he unfurled her scarf and unfastened his high boots. He removed them and jumped onto the bed. He was wearing a blue shirt with a starched collar and wool trousers.

Alice smiled tenderly, loosened his necktie and popped a sweet in his mouth. 'Do you remember that day you slipped and I tickled you... like this?' She extended her hand towards his armpit, but he wriggled away and crossed his arms to protect himself. A squeal escaped him, as though her fingers were tickling him. He pleaded with her. 'Stop. Stop. I'll do anything...'

'Anything?' said Alice teasingly. 'Well then.' She raised her arms above her head and waved them. 'Look. Look. No hands. I'm innocent.'

That gave him exactly the opportunity he needed. He proceeded to tickle her as gently and quickly as possible. Alice, instinctively defending herself from the attack, curled as tightly as she could into a ball. 'Oh God! Save me!' she cried. But Sebastian persisted and he was stronger than she was. He engulfed her in his arms, put out his lips and kissed her cheek. Alice grasped his chin with her right hand and when she kissed him he tasted of pear drops.

As they were lying there together, a new serious look came into his eyes. She searched his eyes for a clue to his changed demeanour.

'I have something to tell you, he whispered.

She had propped herself up on her elbow and was staring at him with intense interest when suddenly she lay back down beside him, as if somehow she knew what he was going to say. Inevitably it was the news she was most dreading. He was going to France again, and this time for six months.

Fearfully and cautiously, Sebastian turned his head from the pillow to look at her, but he found her lost in thought.

All she could see was uncertainty and danger. What madness had forced him to volunteer at the Front was beyond her imagination. The irony was that he was to be stationed near Ypres, that death-ridden, evil place where she had lost Edward. She felt suddenly weak and cold. She drew up the blanket around her shoulders. Would she ever be able to see his face again? With what emotions would she encounter him if he returned? She did not know. She had lost one love in that place. It seemed impossible that she could survive losing another. She did not want to try to picture the world of the unknown, the future. She wanted to anticipate and be in charge of events, not follow them.

She responded in a neutral tone, halfway between interest and disinterest, but it didn't fool either of them. When she asked the questions she dreaded and feared the most, he answered her with a frankness that indicated he understood the gravity of the news he brought, and felt it instinctively.

After he had explained in detail where he would be working and in which field hospital, he lowered his eyes without uttering a word. The silence was hard to bear. He broke it with the only words he could think of that made any sense. 'If I leave again, it will be only because I must come back to you.'

They gazed at each other, hardly able to contain what they were feeling. It seemed to him that her beauty had only intensified with the grim routine and demands of her hospital work. Her hair shone rainbow colours; the curves of her figure appeared even more perfect.

She had wanted to run when he was talking, but now she was just afraid. She returned his kisses, and they allowed her to forget the pain she wished to delete from her memory. A reckless passion seized her that she could no longer deny, yet at the same time she remained haunted by some strange presentiment that this comfort might be short-lived.

For now they could smile at each other and pretend. There was nothing else to say because they had seen this hour, both of them. Both of them saw this chasm, the one they had each dreaded, as inevitable.

They gazed into each other's eyes to reassure the other of reality, one that was not decimated by war, but nourished by love. It said, 'You are you. I am I. Nothing else matters. For the few months of grace we are grateful. Love's embodiment is still alive. Fate has been kind and generous not to separate us sooner.'

She felt his hand squeeze in hers, as though that was enough to express anything else that he might have missed. He no longer seemed to want to talk, as if it was too much effort for him. His eyelids slowly drooped until they closed. Then the lips opened a little and a delicate, recurrent snoring could be heard.

Chapter 11

After a short pause, Kitty said, 'I was wondering if I could ask your opinion about something? It's about Harry Lloyd.'

Kitty had arrived at the apartment dressed in a fur-lined hat and smart blue suit. Her visit was unexpected.

'You have heard from Harry?' said Alice in astonishment.

'Oh indeed! He was wounded, you see. If you could have seen him... the poor lad... I felt so sorry for him.'

'But he's alive,' sighed Alice, still struggling to take in the news.

'He certainly is.... and I am to marry him!'

Alice felt the tears well up in her eyes.

'And do you love him?' she asked.

'Well, he is a decent man...'

'And does he love you?'

Kitty, blushing and confused, said cautiously 'I think so.'

Alice, overcome with her own jostling feelings, spoke from the heart. 'If I have learned anything, it is to grasp whatever happiness comes by us with both hands. You cannot let him go...'

After Kitty had gone she strayed aimlessly into the study where on the desk Grandfather's manuscript still lay in a neat pile. She looked up at the ceiling so that the tears flowed. It would be wonderful to see Harry again, and Kitty had even agreed to give her driving lessons.

Two days later, Kitty brought Harry to tea.

Alice hurried towards him, holding out both hands.

'Alice!' he cried, taking her hand and kissing it.

She turned to Kitty and embraced her.

Harry, oblivious to the enormity of the words he was about to say, blushed scarlet. 'I have something to tell you about Edward...' he said, unaware Alice had quite given up on him. 'I have seen him....'

Alice was forced to sit down. A mask of pain descended over her white face and the news that Hugh had seen Edward so long ago without informing her plunged a knife into her heart. Head spinning, she paced up and down the room, as the realization dawned on her that her oldest friend had betrayed her. The letter for her husband she had once entrusted to his care must never have been passed on.

A little later, in the War Office in Parliament Street, stricken and confused, she clung to the chair arms with both hands, still unable to believe what she had heard. The elderly commanding officer, a large-jointed man named Corporal Frazer, had confirmed Harry Lloyd's account of the events of 1916 in their entirety.

'If Edward is alive, why was I never told?' Alice was speechless with incomprehension, but the question still went unanswered, as did the next.

'I cannot tell you when he arrived in London,' said the officer, 'but he was in Dieppe on the 13th and the Billet Office are the only ones who can tell you which train he caught.'

If the news of her husband was earthshattering, the information that he had visited England only a month earlier was too much to bear.

Seized by an unknown madness, her head began to spin as she contemplated what must have happened. It was as if her soul had cracked open. It lay there in a thousand pieces, laid bare before a total stranger who had never met her or Edward, and who was oblivious to the entire sorry history of the situation.

Somehow she managed to stand. She could hardly feel her legs. She wandered silently and aimlessly along the deep purple-carpeted corridors and out of the building into the street. She managed to make it as far as the Hotel Victoria. There she waited to see the Battalion Billet Officer who confirmed the facts she had been dreading.

Seeking she knew not what, she turned the corner and entered the cavernous concourse of Victoria Station. It was three years since she had waved Edward off, here, on this platform, in almost exactly the same spot by the station clock. She had been twenty-three and married for just four months.

'Mind you don't trip!' Those had been his last words. She could see his face clearly, the doting eyes and smooth chin. She remembered him brimming with optimism, although he could not know what lay in store for him.

Her mind turned instantly to the patients in hospital , unable to help wondering if the injuries she had witnessed there had been inflicted on Edward. The idea filled her with disgust and horror, but it was the thought that he had deliberately abandoned her that tortured her beyond anything else.

Expectant faces peered where the train was drawing in, lumbering with its great burden to platform number eight. Still fretting wildly, she watched the black beast as it huffed into the station, her head filled with voice saying, 'It's not him. It can't be. He won't return to you now, Alice.'

The doors flew open and the men poured out. They looked more like Arctic explorers than soldiers in their sheepskin coats, fur caps and wool hats. Their khaki was black, stained by mud. Some were in rags, bearing rifles and bags, their faces weather-beaten and full of exhaustion.

Pushed by shoulders and elbows, half-expecting to see her husband, Alice's anxious gaze hopped from one to the other, searching for features she recognized as her eyes flitted desperately among the returning groups.

'Edward! Edward!'

The twilight had the shade of a blue lake and the air was soft on the cheek. Bland, indifferent silence replaced the tears, sobs and laughter, but when the crowds had dispersed Edward was nowhere to be seen.

Chapter 12

In the large elegant room a young mother sat beside the fireplace, at her feet a small child. On the hearth rug lay a stumpy-legged, floppy-eared dog that winked at its new allies with both eyes and licked the bone that appeared to be his breakfast.

'There,' said Alice, passing down the remains of a beef paste sandwich, and the little dachshund devoured it.

Eleanor, who had just turned six, patted the silky head, and the dog wagged his tail in acknowledgement of this kind, endearing gesture, giving vent to an affectionate whimper.

Alice, relieved that the packing was finished, stood up and walked into the study. Tea chests and boxes lay strewn across the floor. Trailing her fingers along the mahogany desk, the thought occurred to her how dusty it was. It was almost unrecognizable without the covering of papers, but the leather Chesterfield chair still bore the scratch on the arm and the faint scent of tobacco smoke clung to the tapestry curtains as it had always done.

Her head ached with longing. At the same time she felt nothing but gratitude. She had been blessed with a grandparent who had loved her more than life. She had known great friends and had loved two brave men who had loved her. And now she had been given a new family.

Eleanor gazed at her mother adoringly and the dachshund gazed at her, as if thinking how happy and contented it was that there was anyone in this world who cared for it. Alice had found it wandering in the street one day. Bedraggled and alone, the small dog looked as lost as she felt. Its whiskers were thin, the long sleek fur a little dull and the nose a little grey.

At first she suspected that being a German breed, it had been abandoned or that its owner had been forced out in one of the riots.

She was just thinking how fortunate they were to have found the little dog when, hearing the church clock strike eight, she realized they were late.

She helped Eleanor with her coat and picked up the suitcase. The furniture would be following afterwards. She stood before the cracked, rusted mirror in the hallway and tucked her hair behind her ears. She put on her wide-brimmed turquoise hat, and then straightened the gold brooch on her overcoat.

For a few long moments she was motionless, watching the motes of dust floating like snowflakes in the shaft of light streaming in through the window.

'Come on, my darlings,' she said, taking her daughter's hand, and with that she pulled the door gently behind them.

Outside, the trunk of the car was filled with more leather suitcases that she had packed meticulously and the car prepared for a long journey.

Eleanor let go of her mother's hand and climbed into the back seat.

'Have you remembered your book?' said Alice, who was putting on her driving gloves.

'Yes, mummy. Come on, George!'

Hearing her command, the little dog took its cue, and jumped on to the tartan wool blanket.

After a rough crossing they wound along a lengthier than expected road, passing through Aire-sur-la-Lys, where the surrounding battlefields were still in evidence.

Sitting in the passenger seat, Rose had no idea where they were or where they were going. She complained about the map, insisting on redrawing it, as if it were a vestige of the past. In the back of the car Eleanor sang nursery rhymes. The cold pressed down, but the child was snug beneath the pink blanket with her smiling teddy bear. Beside her on the seat was *The Problems and Solutions to Western Civilization,* although she was not quite old enough yet to read it.

They snaked through the maze of war racked roads lined with skeleton trees whose split, cracked branches held high, as if in defiance. Perhaps they would never heal. Over the brow of a hill the shell-ravaged road turned a bend and curved steeply uphill. Here and there craggy ruins of buildings disintegrated into the tortured land, suggesting where a hamlet had once stood; Bapaume, Clély, Villiers, Brétonneux, Péronne, Grivenes, Hédauville....

Fortunately, the cemetery was relatively easy to find. It lay on the other side of the road in a serene setting shaded by a small copse. Swifts darted in the silver birch trees above the graves, each neat patch planted with daisies and marigold, and marked with a small white cross.

They left the car at the roadside and Eleanor took her mother's hand. They walked ahead, glancing about at the neat, velvety lawn and the row of green poplars that marked the pathway. Rose followed with the little dachshund.

Alice let Eleanor understand that this was where her father lay buried. The child regarded the white cross and the carved name, emitting so little emotion that she might have been thought of as a hardened young soul; but the simple fact was that Eleanor, instead of possessing too little feeling, possessed rather too much and was reduced to a state of silence out of awe as she contemplated the crosses around her. She had been told about the war and the great many men who had died so that she and other children like her might live their lives freely.

Alice stood beside the grave, and the elderly lady led the child towards the wildflower meadow. She was pointing out the birds fluttering among the trees and making chirruping sounds.

Left alone, when there was no one there to see or hear her, Alice wept such tears as if to bear the burden of all the women who grieved. The shadows thrown by the branches felt so dark and still as if they too were in mourning. She watched the clouds that seemed further from the earth than they had ever been, and a pride swelled in her heart that would have stifled even the most desperate of cries.

Five years had passed, but the day Sebastian fell ill was still raw. She remembered how in the madness of it all she had decided to go to him. She recalled the narrow bed like a sea of whiteness. The image of his delirium had crystallized in her memory and she relived how his gaze, directed at the ceiling, had returned to her, as if a tide of peace had swept through him, a curtain high enough to blot out the whole world.

That last day she had kept watch by his side all night, until she was drained of everything except resolve and the dawn light began to filter into the room and his head sank into the pillow, his glistening, pale face peaceful at last.

She fell on her knees and let her fingers touch the grass. The sense of being alone in the world that she had always feared most was beginning to ebb and fade. A calm determination took possession of her and she saw her past as a source of deliverance.

A new Alice had emerged who was full of wisdom. This Alice loved deeply. She knew others were less honest, but she forgave them because, like her, they were only human. She knew she would encounter many defeats, but she would not allow herself to be defeated and she was no longer afraid of anything.

They negotiated a winding, bumpy road where the car lurched drunkenly between the remnants of more yawning shell holes. Rose needed to look at the map again. Slowing beside a crossroads, they stopped to ask directions at a traditional brick farmhouse with gabled windows that must have had a magnificent view across the surrounding countryside. A well-stocked garden, filled with hollyhocks, hyacinths and blue geraniums lay at one side, and there was an apple orchard. The name on the small white sign dangling on the hedge read 'La Maison d'Henri'.

Aurélie, paintbrush in hand, was about to fill in the sky when she caught sight of the car. Still seated on her low wooden stool, she carefully placed the brush in water and looked over.

In the garden a little boy was practising his violin. He was not yet sure of the notes and the melody, just about recognizable as 'Scarborough Fair', was out of tune.

Aunt Marie was putting washing on the line, securing the pegs with her arthritic fingers. She had a clear view of the car.

Some way off in the orchard someone who Rose imagined must have been a farmworker because of his wide-brimmed straw hat and the way he was dressed was deep in concentration picking apples. The man, who did not turn around, seemed to hesitate, as if something had struck him, though he couldn't grasp quite what it was.

Rose paused a few steps away from the front gate and asked in French: 'Can you tell me where I might find the military cemetery at Klein Vierstraat?'

Aurelie gave the directions, smiled cordially and wished her a good day. Rose noticed the gold locket around her neck with and admired it. It was engraved with a smiling angel. The idea occurred to her what a lovely present it would make for Eleanor's birthday.

Sitting in the driving seat at the bottom of the hill, Alice waited patiently for Rose to return. She thought about stepping out to stretch her legs, but decided against it. She was keen to press on while there was still light. Soon it would be Eleanor's bedtime.

Aurélie saw the woman in the car on the road, parked some distance away, her face hidden by her turquoise hat, and the child in the back who turned and waved. She watched the elderly lady return to the passenger seat, and, as they drove off, her eyes followed the car up the hill. She assumed that they were British like her husband. It was a pity that he had lost his hearing or she might have called him over to speak to them.

The car turned off at the junction. Dust hung in the air, as it disappeared over the bare, pitted fields until it grew small and faint, like a stroke in an Impressionist painting.